LIVING PASSIONATELY SERIES

BOOK TWO

The Shepherd's Hook

PAMELA H. BENDER

ISBN: 1494749270

ISBN-13: 9781494749279

Library of Congress Control Number: 2013923387

CreateSpace Independent Publishing Platform

North Charleston, South Carolina

Acknowledgements

Throughout my life I have treasured the opportunity to hear, watch, or read about our soldier's stories during time of war. Their bravery and dedication instilled my respect, appreciation, and admiration for our soldiers. My husband, Joe, my cousin's husband, Rob Adamson, my sons, George Greenslade and Terrance Bender, my grandchildren, Aaron, Christin, and Emily Bender, all served on foreign soil to protect our country. You and all soldiers inspired parts of this story.

Once I retired, our son, Edward Bender, exposed Joe and me to the important work of the 4-H Youth Development Organization. We became leaders to our own 4-H fiber club and enjoyed many years working with 4-H youth. Wendy Stoner and Janet Eastman assisted us as leaders. Thank you for proving that volunteers receive much more than they give. You inspired parts of this story.

During a trip to Dupuyer, Montana, Leanne Hayne and her husband graciously showed us around their beautiful sheep farm, The Beaverslide Dry Goods Company. I will never forget that day and still knit with their magnificent yarn. You inspired parts of this story.

Kathy Davidson is a shepherd and friend. She donated her fleece, let us bring our 4-H members to the farm, and supports 4-H youth at the Sheep to Shawl contests. While speaking to authors at a library, I met Roxanne Dean, another shepherd and friend of Kathy's. On trips to their sheep farm and long dinner conversations with both them and their husbands, Joe and I learned to understand and appreciate sheep. You inspired parts of this story.

Carol Woolcott and her husband, Ron, own The Mannings Shop and teach 4-H youth how to spin and weave shawls. At The Mannings, I bought my own spinning wheel and took classes to learn to spin. Thank you for your patient instruction. You have all inspired parts of this story.

All the fiber artists who raise and enjoy sheep, spin fleece into yarn, and knit, weave, or crochet yarn into clothing, inspired parts of this story. My children and grandchildren who wear the things I knit have kept my interest in this art form alive. Thank you.

Dr. Elizabeth Scarito read the manuscript and offered suggestions. Thank you.

Thank you, Anna and Danny Stoner. Your talent and commitment have given me another beautiful book cover. Anna's natural gentleness was captured by Danny's lens. I am grateful for your inspiring work.

Thank you, Diane Adamson. As always, you have edited and nurtured this story.

I hope you enjoy The Shepherd's Hook.

Dedication

This book is dedicated to

All the brave men and women
who defend our freedom on foreign soil

And

Edward Bender, Wendy Stoner, Janet Eastman
and all 4-H leaders

And

My four friends, each shepherds
to their own flock of sheep or fiber artists

Kathleen Davidson–Potosi Sheep Farm
Glen Rock, Pennsylvania

Roxanne Dean–The Celtic Herd Sheep Farm
Glen Rock, Pennsylvania

Leanne Hayne - The Beaverslide Dry Goods Company
Dupuyer, Montana

Carol Woolcott - The Mannings
East Berlin, PA

One

Bess walked out the front door of the shop and inhaled a deep breath. It was the first warm day in March, and the gentle wind held the tantalizing aroma of Spring's first flowers. Bess stretched her arms over her head and wiggled her fingers in the wind. It felt good, so she continued her exercises to release the tension of the workday.

She bent over at her waist while swinging her arms until finally lowering them to the ground. Her eyes spotted some loose soil and instinctively she scooped up a handful. She squeezed the damp clay, amazed it was actually warm to the touch. *The frost will still be in the ground in Montana, might even have a few feet of snow left*, Bess thought, as she threw the dirt down and brushed her hands together.

As Bess walked down the road toward the Conewago Creek, she thought about the five classmates who'd just completed her course in spinning. The middle-aged women had grown up together so they had kidded, encouraged, and made fun of each other as only best friends can do. Their stories of past escapades had broken the tension that usually stiffens the bodies of first-time spinners. As a result, this group was relaxed and their arms, shoulders, and fingers let the natural flow of the spinning process take over. In just two days, the fiber had passed easily through their light grasps onto their moving wheels. All their spinning wheels had turned in unison, their feet keeping pace as if they were peddling bikes on one of their adventures.

At the end of their lessons, the women had piled into an old van, finding enough room for their new spinning wheels and bags of fiber. Only one large bag of fleece couldn't fit and Olive, the heaviest woman, had stood on the porch refusing to leave it behind. "It'll be gone," Olive had shouted, clutching the bag in her arms. "It's the last one from The Funny Farm."

"It won't fit," one yelled from the car.

"We'll leave you here and they'll haul you away to The Funny Farm," another added, followed by a burst of laughter.

"I'll sit on it," Olive demanded, as she pushed the bag between her friends, then plopped down on top. The shrieks of their laughter had continued to flow out the open windows as the door shut and the car pulled away. Bess had waved and walked back into the shop listening to their dissipating voices as the car sped down the road, over the bridge, and far away.

I had fun teaching them, Bess concluded. *I enjoyed hearing their stories.* She looked around at her new environment where she worked as an instructor. The Mannings Hand Weaving School and Supply Center was even more than the name implied. It was a Mecca for anyone drawn to fiber. It supplied everything a knitter, weaver, or spinner could require including books, workshops, and classes.

I love my new job and Sadie likes her elementary school. Our life on the farm kept us isolated with the memories, she reflected.

Bess stopped and looked back toward the cluster of buildings that made up the shop. It was located in the Pennsylvania countryside south of Harrisburg between Gettysburg and York near the small town of East Berlin. Meadows and farmland surrounded The Mannings.

The original farmhouse stood facing the Conewago Creek and was the home of the owners, Carol and Ron. The shop had been constructed next to the farmhouse and had increased in size to keep up with the expansion of their business.

A driveway led customers between the house and a large barn, which stored the farm's supplies and equipment. The barn was also home to a constantly changing group of cats. They came in various breed combinations, fur lengths, and colors.

Bess counted eight cats and five kittens lying on the blacktop parking lot enjoying the warm rays of the sun. Bess shook her head and smiled. Kittens never lasted very long at The Mannings. Knitters seemed to be as drawn to cats as they were to their craft. The young ones usually ended up being packed up and driven home along with a customer's new yarn.

Across from the barn, the shop's front porch greeted the customers, tempting them to sit in one of the three bentwood rockers. Bess had noticed that it was not uncommon for customers to sit on the porch and rock as they studied their fiber books or cast stitches onto their knitting needles with their new yarn.

Only a few husbands chose to rock upon first arriving. True customers could barely wait to open the front door. Once they crossed its threshold, many customers had likened it to entering paradise. The aroma of lavender, lanolin, and clean skeins of yarn was tempting enough, but the vision of the unlimited shades of color cascading in soft, luxurious fibers took the breath away from most fiber lovers. Tactile customers often spent hours running their fingers over the thousands of skeins of fiber.

Bess turned back to watch the large creek drift by its grassy banks. "I am so blessed to find this place," she whispered. She lifted her face and closed her eyes, letting the sun warm her face. She was at peace, until she sensed it. Through her closed eyelids she had seen the light change as darkness had drifted over her.

The shadow threw her entire body into instinctive behavior, as Bess immediately followed the automatic actions learned back on her sheep farm in Depuyer, Montana. She shaded her eyes and looked up as a huge vulture glided slowly back over her. A cold chill flowed down her spine. Bess searched the sky and spotted three vultures circling above her. She began running full speed down the road toward the bridge. In her mind, however, she was running toward her own pasture, toward her precious sheep or whatever had been wounded and lay dying under the circling watch of the waiting predators.

James and his dog, Shep, were enjoying the ride down the road. James' one hand tapped on the open window frame of his truck, keeping perfect rhythm with the song Toby Keith was singing on the radio. Shep kept his head and one paw outside the other open window and the wind blew his fur and ears up.

"We gotta turn here," James warned his dog. Shep immediately pulled his head and paw in. "Atta boy," James said as he turned. "You betta keep your head in. I don't want you barking at the Jacob sheep we gotta pass." Shep leaned over and began to whimper. "No begging! No barking," James ordered as he turned the corner and started down the road by the farm. Shep whimpered loudly but stayed inside the truck cab as they drove slowly past the sheep, both taking the time to look them over. "Pretty things, aren't they?" James asked his dog. "Last trip Carol told me that they're the oldest breed of sheep, date back to the bible."

He returned his eye to the road and squinted. Shep followed his stare and began to bark. A young girl was running full speed down the road, her long, blonde hair bouncing with each stride. She slowed and her little head tilted up to check something in the sky. Seemingly alarmed by what she saw, she burst into another sprint forward. James stuck his head out the truck window and looked up into the sky. "Vultures," James said to Shep. "Maybe the little girl's afraid of birds."

James drove carefully past the young girl, checking to see if she needed help. She didn't look scared, just damn determined. He knew better than to talk to her, all kids these days were warned not to talk to strangers. He pulled ahead and let her be.

As James neared the bridge, however, he spotted a woman running full force toward the bridge. Her hair was red, long, and flowing behind her as she ran. She wore the same determined expression on her beautiful face.

James stopped the truck and stared in admiration. She didn't cross the bridge but turned and ran into the freshly plowed field. He stepped on the gas and crossed the bridge, pulling the truck up next to the field.

"Stay, Shep," James ordered as he stepped out of the truck and followed the red-haired woman.

Bess spotted the wounded animal, a large calico cat from the barn. She knelt beside it, stroking it gently, helping to distract the cat from the shadows of the vultures. "Hey girl," she said softly. "Let's take a look and see if I can help you." She touched the wounded cat, assessing the damage. Blood was oozing out from her stomach and her behind was covered with clear liquid. "I'm sorry girl," she announced. "I'm afraid it's serious."

"How bad is it?" James asked as he approached the woman.

Bess looked up, surprised by the deep voice of the stranger. The sun was shining directly above him so she couldn't see his face. She looked away from the glare and back at the cat. "It's bad," Bess announced. "It looks like she was hit by a car. I don't know why she crawled off in this direction?"

James knelt beside the cat and did his own appraisal. His fingers felt the limp body, and announced, "Several ribs are crushed and a leg's broken. She got here on pure determination." He was about to lean down to check further when he heard the panting from behind him.

"What is it?" the little girl asked. "Who's hurt?"

"Hi Sadie. Did you run here?" Bess asked.

"Yup. I saw the big, bwack biwds. Knew something got huwt. Oh no!" she said dropping to her knees. "Cricwet, she's my favowite cat. We catch cwickets together; that's why I named hew that. She was going have my kitty," Sadie said, leaning past the stranger to pet the cat.

"Awe you smashed, Cricwet?" Sadie asked in her sweetest voice. She turned and studied the stranger before pointing her finger and asking, "Who's him?"

James looked at the two faces staring up at him. "I'm James from The Funny Farm. I was making a delivery to The Mannings when I saw both of you running toward the field. Figured maybe I could help out."

"Did you say Cricket was having kittens?" Bess asked, ignoring James.

"Yup. I'm waiting fow a giwl kitty. Most wed kitties awe boys," Sadie explained politely to James, as if it was important.

"I see," James said with a slight smile. "You don't like boy cats?"

"I wuvs boy cats but I gots a name for my kittie. Hews gonna be cawwed Miwwie. She's got to have wed hair wike my mommy," Sadie said pointing to Bess.

"Oh, I see," James said, as he looked back at Bess.

"Is that a working sheep dog?" Bess asked, staring toward his truck.

"Yes, that's Shep," James explained.

"Can I borrow him?" Bess asked, as she stood.

"Yes," James said, fascinated by these two females.

"Sadie," Bess said gently, "stay with Cricket. Help her cross over. Mister, would you please stay with her? I'm gonna find those kittens. That's why she dragged herself over here. She had the kittens after the car hit her. Cricket was protecting them from the vultures by dragging herself away."

Bess reached down and grabbed behind Cricket, taking some of the afterbirth in her hand. She stood up, whistled, then yelled, "Come Shep." The dog jumped out the open car window, knowing he was being called to work. Bess ran to meet him, kneeling to let him smell the mucus. "Find them," Bess ordered, and James watched as his dog and the red-haired woman began searching the field.

"She might need my knife. Sometimes the babies are born in the sack and need to be cut out," James said as he watched them move slowly through the field.

"My mom gots a knife aww the time," Sadie assured him.

"Why?" James asked without thinking. He'd never known a woman who carried a knife.

"Cause daddy's dead so Mommie gots it. Ya gots to have a knife. Stuffs needs cutting," Sadie explained patiently, her big, blue eyes growing wider as if in emphasis.

James turned to watch the red-haired widow who was now kneeling down in the field. "I think your mom found the kittens. She might need me to help," he said before looking back at the little girl.

"My momma needs no hewp. She's bownded wots of things. Cwicket needs hewp," Sadie said in an annoyed tone. "Wook, the big biwds want to eat Cwickit!" she urged, pointing up at the huge, raptorial birds swooping above. "We have to stay untiw she dies. I need Singing Bird. Hews knows how to hewp things die."

"What kind of bird is Singing Bird?" James inquired.

"Singing Bird's my fwiend; she's no bird," Sadie answered in growing annoyance.

"Oh," James answered. "Make-believe friends can be great help when you need them."

"Singing Biwd's a weal giwl," Sadie added, as she laid down on the grass so she could look into Cricket's eyes.

James watched in wonder as Sadie began singing Jesus Loves Me to the dying cat. Her hand gently touched the cat's cheek while Cricket nuzzled close to her fingers.

Once the song ended, James suggested, "Maybe Singing Bird will drop by."

"She's not gonna dwop by. She's in Montana 'cause hews a Bwackfoot Indian," Sadie explained, before beginning to sing This Little Light of Mine.

James decided that he'd made enough stupid statements to Sadie so he just sat and continued to stroke Cricket in quiet support.

A loud whistle broke their peaceful mood. Sadie immediately reacted, jumping to her feet and shouting, "Yes, Mamma?"

"I'm sending Shep. Tie your jacket around his neck," Bess yelled. Sadie ran to her backpack, pulled out a pink jacket and waved it. "Fetch," Bess commanded and the dog ran directly to Sadie.

"Good boy," James said as Shep arrived. He helped Sadie tie on the jacket. "Go boy," James commanded and Shep took off back to Sadie's mom.

"The kittens must be alive. She might need your coat to wrap them and keep them warm," James suggested.

"Ya think my wed-haired giwl kitty is bownded? I've been waiting for a wed-haired kitty for a vewy wong time! I weally hope Miwwie's bownded," Sadie said, before kneeling opposite from James.

He watched as one of her little hands stroked the cat and she chewed on the fingernails of the other. Her eyes remained on her Mom. "Not many wed giwl kitties awe awound," she added in case he'd forgotten.

"So I've heard," he said, smiling at the strange, little girl. "I'll bury Cricket after she crosses over. I keep a shovel in the truck."

"No, that's bad. The big, bwack biwds need to eat. Cwickets gonna be in heaven so hews don't cawe if thems eat hew," Sadie said, with the patience of a teacher. "Mom says it's pawt of wife's cycle," and her little, sore finger made a circle in the air.

James stared at the kid, afraid to make one more foolish comment.

James followed Sadie's example and turned to watch the activity in the field. He wasn't prepared for the impact it would have.

The sun was shining down on the neatly plowed rows of dirt, making them look like dark chocolate against the background of lush green on the creek bank. The blue waters of the Conewago Creek were dotted with foamy, white splashes where the water broke on rocks.

Completing the scene, the red-haired woman gently carried a pink bundle in her arms. Her face was glowing with maternal reverence for the new life in her grasp. His dog, Shep, walked at the woman's side as if he'd fallen under her spell. James knew that this would be a moment he would never forget. It was one of those snippets in time when real life was more beautiful than art.

He watched, memorizing all the fine details so that it could be recalled later. While some people took photos, James stayed in the moment, capturing not only the picture but also the essence of the scene. He drew in a deep breath, adding the fragrance to the memory. He listened to Sadie's voice as it sang gently to the dying cat and the vultures' wings as they swooped and flapped above their heads. Then he stared at the woman who approached him.

The sun seemed to ignite sparks of gold in her hair. Her hands were gently placed like a ballerina's during a dance. Her lips formed an expression as difficult to read as that of the Mona Lisa. He couldn't tell if she were smiling or close to crying. Perhaps it was resignation. His heartbeat warned him that she stirred much more than just his artistic talent. She stirred feelings that he had only heard about.

She walked past him, kneeling carefully, and spreading the pink jacket apart so their brave mother could see the five tiny kittens. Then the woman lay down on the grass, her face a few inches from Cricket. She smiled and said ever so gently, "You did it, Cricket. They all survived."

Her words, her pose, her very being touched raw emotion within him. Right there in the field, James Turner felt a strong connection with the brown-eyed woman who lay in the plowed dirt, her face inches away from the nose of a dying barn cat.

Sadie left her position across from James and laid down so that her head touched the top of her mother's. James removed his gaze from the woman and stared at the little girl, noting that her blonde hair had clumps of dirt stuck to it. He studied her little fingernails. They were bitten down, red and raw. Her eyes were crystal blue and where her mom had freckles splattered over her nose, her daughter's skin was smooth and unmarked.

As little as she was, she was the one who had kept James in the loop. Her mother hadn't even acknowledged his presence except to ask him a question and to do a favor. The little one had been the kind and welcoming spirit. He smiled and wondered what these two remarkable beings had experienced to make them the way they were.

Their two faces were even with Cricket's. Their eyes stared back and forth at the cat and the balls of fur that were trying to move. Sadie asked, "Do I see my Miwwie?"

"Yes," her mother answered. "Cricket gave birth to a ginger girl cat. Your Millie has arrived."

Sadie looked over at Cricket as a tear fell down her cheek. She whispered, "You did it! Thank you, Cwicket. I promise I'm gonna wuve hew fowevea and evea."

"We'll find good homes for your other kittens too," Bess promised.

Cricket seemed to understand. James watched her pink tongue make a desperate effort to lick one of her babies, but then her eyes closed and her spirit left. Cricket had crossed over.

James was a man who loved animals. He now dedicated his life to capturing their beauty on canvas and to their breeding, care, and protection. He heard Shep, a dog he deeply loved, begin to whimper in sympathy of Cricket's demise. The entire scene touched James, exposing his vulnerability, and in that instant an involuntary flashback rose from his subconscious. At its arrival, the taste of his own bile burned his throat, his body began shaking, and his breathing became labored. He was back there, lying with his face in the hot sand, his eyes watching in horror as the life left the body lying next to him. "Breathe, God damn it, breathe," he screamed through foggy eyes.

"Are you all right?" Bess asked, as she looked over at the stranger. Her voice penetrated through the past, bringing him back to the present. He glanced at her, gasping and unable to speak.

"Take deep breaths," Bess suggested. "I always do that when I get flashbacks."

"I hummm, they goes away when you hummm," Sadie suggested.

James stared at Bess and saw her warm, brown eyes return to the cat, giving him the privacy he needed. Her daughter tilted her head and smiled at him before looking back to watch the ginger ball of fur. A cool breeze blew over him, confirming he was no longer in the desert. He took the deep breaths Bess had recommended and regained his composure.

When he looked back at their faces, he was grateful that they were still absorbed in Cricket's passing. They seemed more at peace than distraught. After a few minutes, the mother sat up and motioned for Sadie to join her. She lifted the little, red kitten into Sadie's shaking hands and then she stated, "Prophets say, 'death on one level means life on another'. Go in peace, Cricket. You were a good mother."

Sadie smiled and added, "I wuvs Miwwie and she wuvs you. I know it! Thank you for my Miwwie."

They turned to look at James and he cleared his throat and added, "You were one brave cat. You saved your babies."

They all nodded to each other and stood. "Stay Shep," James demanded. "Stay here for a while."

The dog lay down, taking the assigned task to protect the dead cat from the vultures. The three humans walked toward the truck, Sadie carrying Millie and Bess carrying the remaining kittens in the pink coat.

"I'll drive you to The Mannings, drop off my load, and then come back and get Shep. He'll protect her and give time for Cricket's spirit to be gone."

"Good idea," Bess said as she kept her eyes on the little kittens. "I'm not sure we'll be able to save her babies. None of The Mannings' cats can give them care. Only one cat has given birth, and her babies are too little to take off her."

"Momma, what awe you saying?" Sadie asked clutching her kitten.

"I had to cut the sack away from the kittens. Usually their mom chews and licks the sack away. The motion of her tongue stimulates the kittens breathing and circulation. These kittens are barely moving," Bess explained to Sadie.

"I might have a solution," James said as they approached the truck. "I have a cat on my farm whose kittens are old enough to be given away. I could bring these kittens to her and move hers to my house. Tomorrow is Saturday and I'm having friends over, so there's a good chance they'll find new guardians. If not, they can run with the other barn cats."

"Does the cat wanna be momma to Cwicket's kitties?" Sadie asked.

"I hope so. She might adopt them, nurse them like they were hers. Rose has had a few litters and knows just what to do. I'm sure she'll take these little things under her wing," James explained.

"If you would do that," Bess said, "both Sadie and I would really appreciate it." Her gaze remained on the little kittens. "They need your Rose."

"Please Mista James. Hewp my Miwwie, I wuvs her," Sadie begged.

"Climb in and we'll drive up to The Mannings," James suggested.

Sadie sat next to James while Bess sat by the door, the remaining four kittens in her arms. She kept blowing warm air over them. "I can't promise they will live," Bess said to Sadie. "You know it's a real slim chance they'll make it."

"I'm a big giwl," Sadie said sadly. "I know things gotta die." Her little voice began to hum and James realized that she was calling on her own coping mechanism to make it through her fear.

"You can come to The Funny Farm tomorrow and see the kittens. We should know by tomorrow if they're going to be all right. I have an open house for my friends on the last Saturday of every month. There will be lots of visitors, including some kids your age," James announced.

Sadie looked up and asked, "How can Mommy find you?"

"It's on the label on my fleece," James said as they pulled into the driveway. "Fleece is what we call the wool after it's been sheared from the sheep."

"We know that," Sadie said, as her chin jetted up.

"Do you have fleece?" Bess asked suddenly animated.

"Yes, the new spinning teacher has been really good for my business. I wanted to thank her, but I think I'd better get these little ones to my farm."

"I'll get a box for the kittens," Bess said as she climbed out of the jeep, "then I want to see the bags of fleece."

James sat in the car with Sadie as she continued to stroke her little red kitten. She looked up at him and announced, "Mom's the new spinning teachea. Mom wuvs fweece; it's hews thing you know?"

James threw back his head and laughed. "She seems to get all caught up in whatever she is doing."

"Momma does onwy one thing each time," Sadie explained, as she held up one little finger, its nail bleeding just a little. She shrugged and held up two fingers adding, "Hews don't do twos of them. I wait fow Mom to finish with one thing and then she's weady for numba two."

"I'll remember that," James said laughing. "How old are you?"

"I'm six," Sadie explained.

"And your brother and sister?" James asked.

"I has none of them," Sadie said.

"I thought you said your mom born a lot of things," James said, surprised.

"Yup, hews bownded goats, cows, howses, sheep, lots of sheep, dogs, and kitties," Sadie said proudly. "Do chickens count?"

James laughed and it lifted the gloomy mood. He realized that he hadn't had a good laugh in a very long time. It felt renewing. He turned and smiled at the little girl beside him and said, "Chickens count too. Did you live on a farm?"

"Yup. We lived in Montana on a sheep fawm. I hate sheep," Sadie announced, curling her lip up in disgust.

"What? How can you hate sheep? They're kind animals, soft and gentle," James assured the little girl.

"I hate them, but Momma wuvvs 'em. Mama's coming! See you tomowwo," Sadie said, as she slid out of the truck, still clutching Millie.

James stepped out and moved to the back of the truck. He lifted the bags of fleece and placed them on the porch. Then he moved close to Bess, who was placing the kittens in the box. "I want to thank you for your help back there. I don't have flashbacks very often," he apologized.

"We all have memories, some more painful than others. Don't think twice about it," Bess suggested.

Bess turned and walked over to open one bag of fleece. She reached in and gently lifted out the soiled, raw fleece. The aroma, transporting her back to her own flock, transfixed Bess. Her fingers held on tightly to the fleece and tears came to her eyes. "I miss the smell of my sheep," she admitted, as she opened her eyes and lowered the fleece back into the bag. "I'll get the back doors opened and we'll bring them in the shop. I appreciate your help with the kittens," Bess explained.

"I'll see you tomorrow," James urged, before walking away and climbing in his truck.

"I don't even know your name," Bess realized, as the truck started to pull out.

"Ask Sadie. See you tomorrow," James said, as he pulled out.

"Who was that man?" Bess asked.

"Mista James," Sadie explained. "He's nice 'cept fow one thing." She raised one little finger in the air.

"What's that?" Bess asked.

"He has make-bewieve fwiends," Sadie said shaking her head. "He says they hewp him."

"Really? I don't think that sounds too good," Bess said, as they both walked into the shop.

"What if Wose is make-believe," Sadie asked in a very worried tone.

"Let's hope Rose isn't," Bess said, stroking her daughter's hair.

"He wikes sheep," Sadie said.

"He does? He likes sheep?" Bess asked growing more interested. "Seems like you two talked a lot. I'm glad you're talking more. What else did you tell him?"

"I said I hate sheep," Sadie admitted.

"I bet that surprised him," Bess said, shaking her head sadly.

"Trudy, would you open the back doors to the spinning studio? I'll bring the new fleece from The Funny Farm in those doors," Bess suggested.

"Is James outside?" Trudy asked as her hands went directly to her hair. "If he is, we have to tell the other women."

"Why?" Sadie asked.

"Ask your mom," Trudy said with a wry smile.

"I don't know, why?" Bess admitted.

"Because he's the handsomest man any of us have ever seen," Trudy said laughing. "We may all be spoken for but we're not dead." Trudy's eyes grew wide and she shook her head, "I'm sorry, that came out wrong. That was insensitive."

"Trudy, don't worry about it," Bess said, putting her hand on her friend's shoulder.

"Mista James went home," Sadie said.

"Next time, if you see him when he delivers the fleece, you have to let all the women know. We've been waiting for over a week for him to show up," Trudy explained.

"I don't get it?" Bess admitted, as she looked at Sadie and shrugged.

"Did you look at the man?" Trudy asked, exasperated.

"Mama didn't tawk to him much. She was bad. She has one twack in hew head," Sadie clarified.

"She has one track in her brain," Bess corrected and they all laughed. "I never got a good look at him," Bess admitted.

"How long have you been a widow?" Trudy inquired.

"Two years this month," Bess answered, reaching for Sadie's hand.

"It was snowing weal bad," Sadie added.

"Well, spring is warm in Pennsylvania. The flowers are going to bloom, and you should wake up. Life does goes on, doesn't it Sadie?" Trudy asked, smiling at the little girl.

"Yup. I just found my kitten. Cwicket had hew aftew she got smashed. Cwicket saved hew's kitties fwom the big, bwack biwds. She's a hewo. Miwwie's a giwl kitty with wed haiw wike Mamma's," Sadie explained, delight showing on her face. "Mista James took Miwwie home."

"What?" Trudy asked. Now it was her turn to be confused.

Sadie and Bess sat across from each other at their dinner table. Sadie stuck her fork into her macaroni and cheese and looked up at her mom. "I need to tawk to that man. I gotta befowe I go to sweep. I'm so scawed for my Miwwie. Please Mama," Sadie begged.

Bess looked at her watch announcing, "It's six o'clock. If he has a farm, he has work to do until the sun sets. Life on a farm is different from that in a shop," Bess reminded Sadie.

"He's might have a wittwe phone in his pocket," Sadie suggested.

"You're right. I keep forgetting that. We'll finish our supper and then we'll call," Bess said smiling. "I'm as nervous as you. I hope Rose takes our kittens."

"Mama, can we keep more than one?" Sadie asked, her big, blue eyes opening wide.

Bess looked over at her little daughter. Sadie's fingers were in her mouth, and she was biting what was left of her nails. A lump caught in her throat. "The little calico one reminds me of Cricket. I'd like to take her home with Millie. Remember how our Frankie and Johnny played together all the time? Two cats can keep each other company when we're away from home," Bess decided.

"Mama, this is the bestest day ever," Sadie said. She paused and her little face grew sad, "Except for Cwicket getting deaded."

"Sadie, we have to work on your use of words. People in Pennsylvania talk more than we did in Montana. We were out on the farm working. We were lucky we could see each other, remember?" Bess asked her little girl. "No one had those little phones in their pocket in Montana. They didn't work out there."

"We yewwed to each othea," Sadie said smiling.

"We yelled to each other," Bess said. "You repeat it that way. Say er er er er. After a while you'll be able to say the 'r' sound."

"er,er,er,," Sadie said very slowly. "We yewwed at each otherererer."

Bess threw her head back and laughed. "We laughed a lot too," she added.

Sadie jumped up from her chair and ran to her Momma's arms. "We did waugh more than now, Mamma. We gotta waugh more wike when we was home."

"Hello, is this Mr. James?" Bess said, when she heard the phone answered.

"No, its James Turner," the voice answered; a slight chuckle followed.

"I'm sorry. This is Bess Riser, Sadie's mother," Bess added.

"I'm glad you called; I have wonderful news," James said.

"Wait one minute, please. I want Sadie to hear," Bess asked, signaling Sadie to sit on her lap.

"Hi Mistea James. Is Miwwie all wight?" Sadie yelled into the phone.

"Hi Sadie. Rose just loves her. She licked all the kittens from head to toe, then they went to the bathroom for the very first time. That was good; they needed to do that before they could eat. Rose nursed all of them, just like they were her own," James explained.

"Is the cawico one eating too?" Sadie asked. "My mom's going to keep the cawico one 'cause hews wooks wike Cwicket."

"They're all eating and fell sound asleep in a little ball by Rose. I was just milking my goat," James explained.

"You've got goats? I wove goats! I know how to miwk goats, 'caus I did that on ouwa fawm. I weawwy, weawwy wike to dwink goat miwk. I don't get none hewa 'cause they don't got it. Can I dwink a gwass of yow goats miwk when I gets to yowa fawm?" Sadie begged.

"Now Sadie. Don't you think Mr. Turner has done enough for us today?" Bess said gently.

"You finish miwking and I won't ask for yowa goat miwk. Thanks fowevea for taking care of Miwwie and Momma's kitten. What you gonna caww the kitten, Mama?" Sadie asked.

"I don't know yet. Let's leave that for another day. You go get in bed; I'll be in soon," Bess said as she let Sadie down on the floor.

James listened as the little girl ran off. "She's quite a little girl," James said. "I think she's an old soul."

"I can't believe you said that," Bess said, amazed. "The Chief of the Blackfoot Indians once said the same thing about Sadie. Our farm abutted their land and Glacier Park."

"Sounds beautiful. I heard about Singing Bird. At first I thought she had an imaginary friend," James admitted.

Bess started to laugh. She had trouble catching her breath, but it felt wonderful. "I'm so sorry," she finally apologized. "I haven't laughed like that for years. Sadie told me that the only thing she didn't like about you was that you had make-believe friends." They both laughed for a few minutes.

"She's adorable. I even like the cute way she talks," James said.

"Do you mind if I call you James?" Bess asked.

"Don't call me Mr. Turner. It would make me feel like an old man," James said.

"I must admit. I wouldn't know how old you are or what you look like. I was totally wrapped up in saving the kittens," Bess explained. "It seems the women in the shop think you're the most handsome man they've ever seen. They were mad that I didn't tell them you had brought the fleece."

They both laughed. "Let's face it, Bess. How many men come to your shop?" James said with another chuckle.

"You seem to be a very good man. You should know that Sadie stopped talking for almost two years. She just started talking again a month ago. She's still fragile. You can't imagine what this little kitten means to her. I think she started talking because she knew Millie was coming soon. It sounds crazy, I know," Bess admitted.

"Not at all. I've heard old souls know things like that and they feel things deep inside," James responded.

"She's still a little girl, a very hurt little girl. We both have a long way to go," Bess said sadly. "Thanks for your help today. What time should we come tomorrow?"

"Anytime. My friends show up at the farm all day and some camp here. They bring guitars, banjos, and marshmallows. We sing around the fire at night. It's a monthly tradition on The Funny Farm. I have to warn you," James said seriously. "People have been known to leave with all kinds of critters like rabbits, chicks, ducklings, lambs, and puppies. Warn Sadie that she can't bring anything home until Millie and Callie are ready to go home."

"Callie? Did you name the kittens already?" Bess asked.

"Yup. All animals have names on my farm, even my sheep," James admitted.

"Mine did too," Bess added. "I like that name. I'm gonna keep my kitten named Callie. We'll bring marshmallows, and I might bring my spinning wheel. The kids might like to see how the sheep's wool turns into yarn. Do you think they'd like that?" Bess asked.

"It sounds like a great idea. We've never had a spinning wheel on the farm," James admitted. "By the way, you must be the spinning teacher whose been ordering more fleece from our farm. Thanks."

"I think your fleece is the best, especially for new students. The length of each fiber is so long and the curl is perfect. I hope I can spend some time with your sheep. I've never been around Blue-faced Leicester before. I raised merino sheep on our farm. I miss mine," Bess explained.

"I'd like to hear more about them," James emphasized. "Tell me, Bess. Is there some reason Sadie is afraid of sheep. I can't imagine why when she's fearless about everything else," James asked carefully.

"She's not afraid of sheep. She's mad at them. As angry as one little girl can ever get, but thanks for asking," Bess explained, and then there was quiet. "I can't talk about it. It's still too hard to talk about."

"I apologize, didn't mean to pressure you. Thanks for the heads up. The Funny Farm is designed to be a safe place where every-body can forget their problems, pains, or past. You two should have fun tomorrow," James promised.

"That's just what we need," Bess said. "A safe place with just friends, no questions, and no expectations. Now I can't wait. See you tomorrow," Bess said and hung up very slowly.

"Is Mista James mawwied?" Sadie asked as Bess tucked her in and sat on her bed.

"I think so, why?" Bess asked.

"Why do you think he's mawwied?" Sadie asked.

"Because he talks like a married man. He says things like *we* and *our farm*," Bess explained. "I feel more comfortable with him because he is married. The last thing we need is someone getting into our lives. We have to just focus on each other and our new kittens," Bess said gently.

"You focus on one thing, I'm gonna think about aww things," Sadie decided. "How long befowe my Miwwie comes home?"

"I think ten weeks should be long enough, especially since we will have two kittens to keep each other company," Bess said.

"Now honey, we have to talk about something else. Mr. James said that there would be lots of people at the farm. He doesn't have pretend friends; he just thought Singing Bird was your pretend friend," Bess said.

"I wike him better now," Sadie admitted.

"There will be lots of critters on the farm. I want you to promise not to ask me to take any home. We have to wait for our kittens. We only have a small yard here. We're lucky our landlord lets us have kittens," Bess emphasized.

"Mamma, yous the one that wants cwittas. Yous always wants more cwittas," Sadie said, lifting her arms out of the blankets. "Can you leave cwittas at the fawm?"

"I don't know," Bess said honestly, shaking her head slowly. "I just don't know."

"What if they have a tiny, wittwe goat?" Sadie teased.

"Oh no, not a tiny, little goat. Is it one we could milk someday?" Bess asked, loving the game.

"Yup." Sadie teased, shaking her finger.

"I could try to leave it," Bess said.

"What's if thewe is a woosta? And chickens?" Sadie asked, her eyes growing wider.

"I could never leave behind chickens, and you know how I love roosters?" Bess said, lying down and covering her face with a pillow."

"What if hims got a wwama, just like our wwama, Juan?" Sadie asked quietly.

"Then I'd show respect for that llama and the work he is doing. I'd never try to pet him, but I would let him see that I think he's very special," Bess said sadly.

"What if he's spits at us?" Sadie asked.

"Then I'd know we both got too close," Bess said, before reaching for Sadie and giving her a big hug.

"Me too. I wuuv wwamas," Sadie whispered into her mom's ear

"So do I," Bess answered and they both began to cry.

Four

"Wake up sweepy head," Sadie whispered as she shook Bess.

"What time is it?" Bess moaned rolling over.

"I'm just a kid. I can't teww time," Sadie said, right before Bess grabbed her and dragged her into bed.

"Let me look," Bess whispered, after kissing her little girl's cheek. "It's six o'clock, and it's Saturday. We could try to sleep a little longer."

"We sweep too long. We got to go see Miwwie and the kitties," Sadie said looking into her mom's eyes. "If we was on owa fawm, I'd have owa eggs by now."

"If we were on our farm, I'd have our eggs by now," Bess repeated slowly. "Now you say it that way."

Bess listened as her little girl repeated the corrected sentence. Sadie finished and looked up with a proud smile. "I'm getting it, wight?" she added

"Almost perfect. We still need work on your 'r' and 'l' sounds," Bess said gently. Sadie shut her mouth and dove under the covers, snuggled next to her mom. "Too much coaching?" Bess asked. She felt the little head shake *yes* against her shoulder. "Does your speech teacher work with you every day?" She felt Sadie's head sign *yes.* "Then today is just a day to rest and play. Want to sleep some more?" Bess felt her head shake *no.* "Why not?"

Sadie's little face emerged from under the covers. "We gots to go to the fawm to miwk the goat," Sadie implored.

"You don't know if Mister James' goat will let you milk her like yours did," Bess warned.

"I wuvved my goat," Sadie said sadly.

"I have a name for my new kitten. Want to hear it?" Bess asked hopefully.

Sadie sat up and clapped her hands, yelling, "Yes."

"Her name could be Callie. Do you like that? Then it would be Millie and Callie," Bess said, watching her daughter's face as she took in the information.

Sadie smiled, took a deep breath, and thought before speaking, then she said, "I wuuvs it."

"And I love you," Bess said, touching the tip of her finger to her nose. "We could wake up and bake some cupcakes for Mr. James' friends. Would you like that?"

Sadie was out of bed and running down the hall. "Chocowate cupcakes with white icing," she yelled back to her mom.

"We didn't bake enough cupcakes," Sadie said, as they pulled up to The Funny Farm. They both stared at the line of cars that was waiting patiently to park.

"You're right," Bess agreed.

"I'm not tawking no mowe today," Sadie announced, as she looked at the crowd of strangers.

"Don't worry about fixing anything today. Mr. James told me that The Funny Farm is designed to be a safe place where everybody can forget their problems, pains, or past."

"Weally?" Sadie said, her eyes opening wide. "I can tawk here?"

"Don't you talk at school?" Bess asked, shocked.

"Nope. I don't tawk at school yet," Sadie admitted.

"Do you have friends?" Bess asked.

"Yup. Most giwls tawk, not wisten," Sadie said with a smile. "I gots wots to wisten to."

"You talk today and practice so you can start to talk at school too," Bess said hopefully.

A tall, brown-haired woman signaled them to move forward. She wore jeans, a red flannel shirt, and a big welcoming smile. She was absolutely beautiful. Bess rolled down her window and smiled up at the woman. "Welcome. Names please," the lady asked.

"Bess and Sadie Riser," Bess announced, as she watched her check the list. "Great! Looks like James told you the rules."

"I don't think he did," Bess said growing confused.

"Enjoy yourself," the woman said laughing. "That's the main rule. Nice to meet you. I'm Ginny Turner," she announced as she extended her hand to greet Bess.

"It's nice to meet you. Is this by invitation only?" Bess asked.

"Sure is and James wants a list of all guests on the farm. He feels responsible to watch over everyone while they're here. Wants to make sure no one gets hurt or lost. We have several hundred acres, some in woods," Ginny explained. "It's a shepherd thing. They always protect their flock." She shrugged and smiled.

Bess felt as though she'd been slapped across the face. She froze and tears formed in her eyes. Ginny noticed the raw pain and asked, "Are you all right?"

"No," Bess answered, as she turned to look at her daughter. Sadie had covered her face with her hands and Bess could hear her crying. "I think we have to go. It's too soon."

"No, don't. Pull to the side, please" Ginny asked. She turned and yelled, "Take over, Jim. I have to take a break." Then she gently asked, "Can I drive? I know a good place to park. If you want to leave after we talk, you can still get out."

Bess slid over and Ginny sat behind the wheel. "Your kittens are so cute," she said as she slowly pulled forward and headed away from the row of cars and up the dirt road.

Sadie took her hands away from her face and sniffed before asking, "What about my wed-haiwed giwl kitty?"

"She's so lively. James told me her name is Millie," Ginny said as she pulled to the crest of a small hill. "Welcome to The Funny Farm," she said proudly, as Bess and Sadie took a long look at the farm.

"It looks like Heaven's Gate" Bess said softly.

"What a nice thing to say," Ginny said.

"Heaven's Gate was the name of our farm," Bess explained. "Except we abutted the Rocky Mountains and Glacier Park in Montana."

"We're next to the state parkland and some Pennsylvania hills," Ginny explained. "There's the barn with your kittens."

"Don't move yet, please. Tell me more about your farm," Bess asked.

"The Funny Farm has lots of strange animals on it. James can never say *no*. Anytime someone needs to find a home for a critter that doesn't fit on their land, they call him. Everything sort of fits here."

Ginny pointed toward the sheep grazing on the hills, adding, "He raises Bluefaced Leicester sheep. He stays with fiber sheep so he can keep the majority of the animals throughout their lives. The flock keeps getting bigger."

"I can imagine," Bess said as she stared at the few hundred sheep. "He keeps all the lambs too?"

"Afraid so. He can't seem to send anything to the butcher," Ginny explained with a chuckle. "James designed the farmhouse and had it built. It's almost done. All it needs is a coat of paint. You'd think he'd have done that long ago since he's a painter," Ginny said shrugging.

"He paints houses too?" Bess asked.

"No, he's an artist. He's quite well known. His work is always in demand. His studio is in that tree," Ginny explained as she pointed toward a huge, oak tree with a brightly colored tree house. "James does things differently. He's a unique individual."

Bess followed to where she was pointing and gasped. The tree house was not unlike the explosion of color in the yarn shop. Shades of all seven prime colors flowed like water from the roof, down the walls, ending in drops on the huge, oak tree.

It was the size of a small house, little rooms extending onto different branches. A chimney suggested that a fireplace might be inside. A strong, sturdy set of steps led up to the studio. It was imaginative, unconventional, and absolutely perfect.

"A twee house?" Sadie said almost gasping. "Could I go up in it?"

"No," Ginny said. "That's off limits. No one but James ever goes there. He lived there for two years while they built the house. We all thought he'd paint the house to match the tree house, but he hasn't. He says he's waiting for something to inspire him." She shrugged again and added, "There are only a few places off limits on the farm. And a few animals."

"Let me guess," Bess said laughing. "I see a guard llama. I bet he's off limits."

"Sure is, but it's a girl," Ginny announced. "James read research that showed female llamas are better protectors for sheep. He named her Big, Bad Bertha." Everyone laughed.

Bess expected Ginny to ask if their farm had a llama. The question never came. "I'm getting the feeling that no one asks questions on this farm," Bess suggested.

"That's right. We all have to answer too many questions every day. Here people only share what they want and everyone listens without judging," Ginny explained.

"Is this a religion?" Bess asked, growing concerned.

"No and it's not a cult," Ginny said. "We follow the rules that James' unit devised while they were fighting in the desert in Afghanistan. It's really a wonderful way to avoid stress," Ginny admitted. "It's like taking a breather from the world one weekend a month."

"I think we can stay then," Bess said relaxing. "What do you think, Sadie?"

"There's wots of sheep," Sadie said. "I do hate sheep." The car grew silent, until finally Sadie announced. "I want to see my kitten and I do wove goats. Did Mista James miwk the goat yet?"

Ginny checked her watch and announced, "No, it's only 9:45. He's gonna milk the goats at 11:00. He told me you can milk one if you'd like," Ginny added.

"I can? Weally and twully?" Sadie asked.

"Really and truly," Ginny said laughing, and Bess knew instantly that she'd found a friend.

"Thank you," Bess said. "Sadie had her own goat, and she milked it every day." "How wonderful," Ginny said.

The car grew silent until Sadie added, "My goat was named Agnes, and she was the best goat ever. Agnes gave two gawwons of miwk a day. I miss dwinking Agnes' miwk."

"James told me that today you can drink a big glass of Dipsy's milk, but I don't think it tastes good. Dipsy is very gentle. She'll be glad to have you milk her," Ginny explained.

"It's quiet," Sadie whispered as they walked into the small barn.

"This is another place no one is allowed to come. Since you have animals here, you can come inside. This is the barn where James will put the new mothers and their sheep after they lamb. Since the flock is so large now, he read that the mother needs to bond with her babies and feel them nurse before they can return to the flock. If she doesn't do that, she won't know they're hers and she won't nurse. Lambing hasn't started yet, so now only Rose, your kittens and The Mad Hatter are here," Ginny explained.

"I don't think all his lambs will fit in here if they come close together," Bess said, growing more concerned.

"I don't know much about the sheep," Ginny admitted. "There's the Mad Hatter."

Bess and Sadie looked over to where she was pointing. "The Mad Hatter?" Bess asked looking around. "What is it?"

"He's a little, adorable Nubian donkey. Nubian donkeys have a cross on their back. There's a legend why," Ginny said, as she walked over to the pen in the corner. "See, he's cute as can be, only a few weeks old, but the meanest thing ever. He doesn't deserve that cross."

Sadie tiptoed up to peek between the boards on the donkey's stall. She ended up looking directly into his big, brown eyes.

"What's the story?" Bess asked, as she studied the little thing.

"The legend goes that a donkey carried Mary to Bethlehem on her way to Egypt to have baby Jesus, and it had a cross on his back. A Nubian donkey with a cross carried Jesus to Jerusalem on Palm Sunday," Ginny added. "This one is a rascal. He's only good to protect the sheep, wants nothing to do with any people. Bites and brays like a rusty hinge if you get near him. James keeps him here when people come to visit."

Sadie kept staring at the little donkey. The little girl felt as though he was calling to her to come closer. She slipped three fingers through the slot in the stall fencing. The Mad Hatter moved closer to the stall door. Sadie smiled and pushed her entire hand toward the donkey.

"Don't," Ginny said as she noticed.

The Mad Hatter and Sadie ignored her. The little donkey came over to Sadie's hand to smell her fingers. Then, ever so gently, it began licking her red and raw bitten fingernails. "He's not The Mad Hattea," Sadie said giggling. "He's Wascal, a sweet, wittle boy."

"Rascal really likes you," Bess said laughing.

"Should I open the door and see what happens?' Ginny asked Bess.

The two women looked as Sadie put her face as close to the opening as possible. "Hi Wascal," she whispered. "Have you been waiting fwa me?"

Rascal leaned forward and licked her nose. Then he took two steps back and began braying toward Sadie.

"He wants me," Sadie said. "Pwease open the doowa."

"Okay, let's open it," Bess said softly and looked at Ginny. "Maybe they have a connection."

Ginny swung the door open and Rascal trotted directly up to Sadie. Sadie put her arms around his neck and whispered into one of his huge ears, "I'm Sadie. Evewething is going to be aww wight."

Bess and Ginny watched in amazement as Rascal's eyes closed and a look of peace stilled his little body.

Twenty minutes later, Rascal followed Sadie to visit the kittens. They were snuggled against Rose and only awoke when Rascal delivered his loud, heehaw greeting. Sadie sat down on the clean bed of hay and reached for Millie. Rascal lay down next to Sadie, placing his head on her lap. Bess sat on her other side and picked up Callie.

Ginny whispered to Bess. "I've got to go help park cars. You can leave your car right here. It's closer to unload your spinning wheel. James told me you might do a demonstration later. Keep your eye on Rascal. I can't quite believe he's transformed."

"I will," Bess whispered. "It's 10:15. We'll find the goat area before 11. Thanks so much."

"Mama," Sadie whispered. "I know Mista James is not mawwied."

"That's his wife," Bess said shaking her head. "Are you trying to fix me up so you can visit Rascal more?"

"Nope. I know 'cause his house isn't painted," Sadie announced.

Bess was busy looking into Callie's blue eyes. Her one track mind was only on her kitten now, as she whispered, "Hello Callie. You're all mine."

Sadie looked into the yellow eyes of her Millie. "You are my baby. This is Wascal," Sadie said as if her kitten could understand. Millie licked Sadie's nose and when Sadie put her on Rascal's back she moved up to lick the little donkey's big, brown nose.

Five

"I had to come and see for myself," James said, as he walked into the little barn. "Sadie, have you tamed that beast?"

"Wascal's no beast," Sadie reported, smiling up at James. "I wuuvs him and he wuuvs me."

Bess smiled up at the man adding, "Please excuse her. She doesn't know that love doesn't happen that quickly." She shrugged and started to get up.

"Sit," James said. "I want to see the little ones." He sat between the two of them and leaned forward to pick up the black kitten. James nuzzled his nose against its stomach. "This one is mine because he's the only boy. I'm gonna call him Junior." He turned to stare at Bess, "I believe love happens just that way. It hits people between the eyes and in the heart. They never see it coming."

"Likes an awwow fwoms an angew," Sadie added, and they both smiled at Bess.

"I didn't know angels had arrows," Bess said laughing.

Bess turned her gaze from her kitten and looked directly at James. She studied him, analyzing every detail. "You are the handsomest man I ever saw," she declared. "I'm trying to figure out what makes you that way. Your nose is nice, your ears are perfect, nice skin, and great blue eyes. Your blonde hair shows it all off. The women at the shop are right; you've got it all. I wonder if Ginny still sees you that way."

"No, Ginny never saw me that way, thank God. If she had, she'd only be looking at the proportions of my face."

"I see what you mean, like I just did, but your features fit together perfectly," Bess decided.

"As you probably guessed from my tree house, I'm a painter. People are always judging things by what scientists and artists call 'the divine proportion'. If they think they see it, they feel comfortable and call it good looking," James explained. "It's really all math."

"I like math. I can count to one hundwed," Sadie said, proudly.

"Well, look at my eye," James said as he turned to face Sadie.

"Bwue wike me," Sadie observed. "Mama's are bwown wike Wascals." Everyone laughed.

"Great, I look like an ass," Bess said shaking her head.

"Watch this, Sadie. If I pull my cheek and lower my eye just a little, what does it look like?"

"Bad," Sadie decided, shaking her head.

"See you want it to be where you think it should be, but I'd still see just as good if my eye was a little lower on my face," James explained. "So how people look is not important. I like to paint people whose faces are just off enough to be interesting."

"Wike mama! She's has spwotches of wed on hews nose," Sadie said laughing.

"I think her freckles are interesting and make her look unique," James said, looking toward Bess.

"So now I'm interesting because I'm a splotchy faced mother with eyes like an ass," Bess said shrugging. "You two are are not very good for my ego."

"Yous pwetty, Mamma," Sadie insisted.

"You certainly are," James agreed. "I'd like to paint you someday."

Bess blushed and moved back. "No, I'm not a model, just a mom. You and your 'divine proportions' should model."

"I think that's a compliment," James said.

"Nope, just a mathematic observation," Bess said, lifting one perfectly arched, red eyebrow.

James turned to Sadie. "What should we do with your new friend, Rascal? Is that his name now?"

Sadie looked down as the little donkey and asked him, "Are yous Wascal?"

The donkey answered with a hilarious heehaw sound. Bess shook her head and James slapped his knee announcing, "Rascal it is. I'm not sure how Rascal will act around the other kids. Do you think we should let him stay here while we go milk the goats?"

"No," Sadie said, without hesitating. She looked down, shaking her head, saying nothing. James turned and put one hand on her shoulder.

"Sadie, you never have to rush when we talk. Take your time; think it out. I will never leave until you say what you want, just the way you want," James assured her.

Sadie pointed to herself and whispered, "I need him." Her little finger with its bitten down, nubby nail ended up on Rascal's wet nose.

"Well said," James announced. "He's yours whenever you come. Take him where you want."

Sadie smiled and leaned over to kiss the little donkey's head. "Miwwie needs Wose," Sadie said, with carefully chosen words.

"Yup. She needs to eat and sleep right now. So do Callie and Junior. We have to go milk a few goats," James announced.

"Dipsy's a goat! Wight? Miss Ginny said so," Sadie asked.

"Right, and you can milk Dipsy if you want," James explained.

James, Bess, and Sadie placed their kittens by Rose and smiled when she licked and checked them over. "She's a good mama like you," Sadie said very carefully.

"Thanks, honey," Bess said taking her hand, as they all walked through the barn. Rascal trotted happily behind Sadie.

"When Ginny called to tell me about Sadie and Rascal, she told me how much she liked the name of your farm," James reported.

"Heaven's Gate," Bess said softly. "Your farm reminds me how much I loved it." Bess looked out onto the field of grazing sheep. "To work alongside nature is the best job in the world." She took in a deep breath. "I love the smell and sounds of a farm. Only a farm can fill all your sensory needs. And the animals, to be loved by so many living creatures is intoxicating."

"Mama aways wants to take cwitters home. Daddy had to say *no* sometimes," Sadie warned. A thought crossed her mind and she tugged the corner of James's shirt. He bent down and looked into her blue eyes. Sadie took in a deep breath and slowly asked, "Can I keep Wascal? Can he wive with me?"

"Rascal would miss his sheep. He loves to be with them. He'll grow up and guard them with Big, Bad Bertha," James explained.

"Does you have beaws?" Sadie asked, as terror froze her body.

"No grizzly bears," Bess said, turning Sadie towards her. "No grizzly bears live in Pennsylvania."

"No grizzly bears," James said, intrigued by the exchange.

"I hate beaws. I don't want Wascal guawding yoas sheep," Sadie yelled, as she ran back into the barn. Rascal followed her, jumping and running as fast as his little legs could go.

"You go milk the goats. I'll take care of Sadie," Bess announced.

"I'm sorry. I don't know what frightened her," James admitted.

"It's a long story. Thank you for taking so much time from your day. Please, I don't want to make you late," Bess urged. "I'll go to Sadie."

James stood and watched as Bess ran into the barn. He brushed his hair back from his forehead thinking, "I wonder what they're running from?"

Bess found Sadie holding Millie, the little donkey standing behind her. As she approached, Rascal curled back his lips and began braying loudly, warning her away. Bess smiled and said, "Sadie, look at that donkey! It's a baby and look how fierce it is already. It's going to grow to be four feet tall, almost as big as a horse. It'll have big, long ears and kick harder than a mule. You'll be able to ride that thing. That donkey needs to have a job. It likes to protect things. Don't worry, honey. There are no grizzly bears in Pennsylvania."

Sadie turned and watched the little jackass. She began to laugh at the loud, weird noises it was making. "Tell him I'm a friend," Bess said laughing with her daughter.

"Stop Wascal," Sadie said, gently touching his back. "That's momma."

As they walked through the crowd of people, they were greeted with comments like "good morning", and "like your ass."

"Which way to the goats?" Bess asked.

"Follow us; we're on our way," one mother said as she walked with her daughter.

"I like that thing. Is that your donkey?" the older girl asked.

"He wuuvs me," Sadie said.

"Do you think he'd love me?" the girl asked.

"You try," Sadie suggested, and they stopped.

"Hi there," the girl said as she reached her hand toward Rascal. He curled up his lips and showed his teeth braying loudly.

"I think he only likes you," the girl announced.

"I thinks so," Sadie agreed.

"You're cute. I'm eight years old," the stranger announced.

"I'm six. I'm not tawking so good yet. I just started tawking again," Sadie admitted.

"You can practice with me," the girl suggested. "I'm going to be a teacher. You can pretend to be in my class."

"I tawk swow," Sadie said.

"You should sing," the older girl decided. "Do you know any songs?"

"Not many," Sadie admitted.

"I know lots," the eight-year-old bragged. "My name is Judy. I'll teach you. Can you jump rope? I know lots of sayings for jumping rope. I can teach you."

"Good, but I got to miwk Dipsy," Sadie said.

"We're going to watch Mr. James milk. Are you really going to milk a goat?" Judy asked.

"Yup, and dwink a gwass of goat miwk," Sadie said proudly.

"Yuk," Judy said making a face.

"Yum," Sadie said laughing.

Bess sat on the grass with Judy's mother, watching as Sadie and her new friend sat cross-legged playing patty cake. "Your daughter's broken through Sadie's walls. I just found out that she doesn't talk to the girls at school," Bess confided to Judy's mother.

"Little Sadie doesn't have to worry about how she talks when she's here. The kids think she's the best," the mother said smiling. "Not only does she have a cute little donkey that likes only her, but she knew just how to milk the goat. The best part was when James poured some milk from the pail into a glass, and Sadie drank it down. I thought the kids would throw up." The two women laughed.

"Where did all the men go?" Bess asked. "I saw them pile into the wagon behind the tractor and take off for the woods."

"They're cutting down trees for the games," the woman explained.

"Games?" Bess asked.

"It's March. They all get to play lumberjacks. They have all kinds of races. They'll split logs, climb poles and roll logs in the lake. They even have team races. They'll carry pine poles that weigh close to 1500 pounds. They can't help themselves. They'll all hurt next week, but today they'll never admit it. They go right back to being Special Forces in their heads," the woman explained. "You know, they don't feel the pain; they push through it."

"All of them Special Forces?" Sadie asked.

"Retired from the same platoon. They're like family to each other. Most wouldn't miss a month without seeing their Captain," she explained.

"Who's the Captain?" Bess asked.

"Why, James. Didn't you know that? He's a hero," she said smiling. "Didn't your husband tell you about him?" the woman asked.

Bess shook her head sadly, her hand reaching down to touch her wedding ring. "I'm a widow," Bess whispered.

The woman reached out and took Bess into her arms. "I won't ask any questions, but I am so sorry. I'm Fran. I have your back," she whispered.

During the next hour, Fran explained the different ceremonial activities for the upcoming months. "Last month we helped with the shearing. Most of his men were taught how to shear. April is lambing month, of course," she advised. We all try to help out, but James has his hands too full. We can't help as much as I wish we could."

"I thought most lambing was done in March," Bess said. "Why so late on The Funny Farm?"

"This farm connects to the State Forest. Early spring the black bears come out and they're very hungry. They'd kill and eat his lambs. They're so desperate for food they'll even fight Big, Bad Bertha for a lamb. He plans his lambing to be a month later. By then most of the bears have eaten enough that they don't want to face that big llama. The lambs are fairly safe," Fran explained.

"Please don't mention bears to Sadie," Bess asked, grabbing Fran's arm. "Please."

"I won't. I'll tell Judy not to either," Fran promised, noting the tears in Bess' eyes. "Sadie must feel protective over sheep."

"No way," Bess answered "She hates sheep."

"You love sheep and she hates them. You must have some story to tell," Fran said gently.

"Unfortunately, we do, but both of us can't talk about it yet," Bess said. "Would anyone be interested in a spinning demonstration? I brought my spinning wheel?" "Absolutely. We'd love to see what happens after the wool leaves this farm," Fran admitted.

The demonstration lasted two hours and finally Bess stopped her wheel. As the crowd dispersed, she asked Fran. "I have to take my wheel back to the car. Would you mind keeping an eye on Sadie and Rascal?" Bess turned to look out at the flock of sheep. "We used to have a sheep farm, and I'd love to spend some time with them in the field after I take my wheel to the car. It would mean so much to me," Bess asked.

"Of course. I'd do anything to help you. Just ask, please. Besides, our daughters and that donkey are tied at the hip." Fran assured her.

"I'm going to take a walk to see the sheep," Bess said to Sadie. "Miss Fran will watch you."

"I'm teaching her," Judy said smiling.

"I am herrrrr student," Sadie said very carefully.

"Good job, honey," Bess said, before turning and walking away from the noise and laughter.

Bess walked down the path, past the barns, through the gate and into the pasture. The llama, Big, Bad Bertha, came running toward her, stomping her feet and making a loud snort. Bess smiled and extended both hands palms up, careful to keep her head lower than the llama's. Big, Bad Bertha stomped her hoofs and slowly Bess lifted her face and smiled. The huge llama walked around her, stomping and snorting.

"Hi Bertha," Bess said gently. "You're doing a good job, girl. Can I go see your sheep?" Bess asked.

Bertha lowered her nose and smelled Bess' hand. "I know, girl. Right now, I smell like donkey, kitten, and goat; but I love sheep as much as you do. Can I visit your flock?" Bess asked.

Big, Bad Bertha looked down at Bess, snorted and trotted back to her sheep. She turned and watched as Bess followed her.

"You sure look different," Bess said as she neared the flock. "Look at those faces! You look like little, Greek soldiers." The females followed the lead of the alpha sheep edging slowly toward Bess.

"Hi there, girl," Bess said as she reached out to pet the head of the first sheep. "Aren't you a lovely ewe," Bess cooed as she patted her head. The sheep didn't move away, instead, they surrounded her. "Tears formed and fell down her cheeks. "You girls will soon be mommies," she whispered. "I miss being with my sheep, so I'm sure happy to see all of you."

The wagon was headed down the hill about to exit the woods when James stopped the tractor. He stared in wonder at the scene before him.

"You okay, Cap?" one man called from on top of the wagon full of logs.

"Just didn't want to scare the sheep while they're surrounding Bess," James said gently.

"That lady sure likes sheep," one man said.

No one asked further questions. They didn't need to. They knew James better than he knew himself. They could see it all on his face, hear it in his tone, when he simply said, "She's special, that one."

"Mama, are they gonna hurt each other?" Sadie asked, burying her head under her mother's shirt.

"No honey, its just a game they play, like football," Bess said, but she was shocked too.

"We's not gonna pway, are we?" Sadie asked from under the shirt.

"No way. I think it's too hard. Maybe they shouldn't even try this," Bess said, as the teams grunted and hauled huge poles up the hill.

"Don't worry about them" Fran urged. "This isn't hard for these men. They've survived much worse."

"How does this work?" Bess asked. "Who can win?"

"They all win if they all get their poles to the top," Fran explained. "They're not competing against each other; they're competing against themselves. My husband says they're battling against giving up."

"What's that noise?" Bess asked.

"At the front of each pole, an officer leads his team. He has to know the pace that will get his men across. The men give him information, calling out, *all's good* or *ease up*. He listens and counts out the pace," Fran said.

Bess watched as five teams of ten men began moving their heavy load up the steep, grassy hill. It had taken the women and kids half an hour to scale it, the youngest on their hands and knees. Bess was still panting from the steep climb, her heart beating fast within her chest. She stared at the rows of muscular, he-men. They were still in top physical shape, their muscles bulging under the load. "That's a lot of testosterone," Bess proclaimed.

"It's the best show in town," Fran said, nudging Bess and laughing.

"The women in the shop would love to see this," Bess said. "How'd I get so lucky?"

Fran looked at Bess surprised, and then admitted, "I just assumed your husband had been in the platoon."

"No. We met James yesterday while he was delivering fleece to the shop where I teach spinning. A cat had been hit by a car, and Sadie and I were trying to help her," Bess explained, as her daughter's head popped from under her shirt.

"Cwicket was hew's name. She had babies. She bownded me Miwwie," Sadie announced. Mama's gonna keep Cawwie and James' gonna keep Juniorrrr.

"James' cat adopted them," Bess added. "They're here on the farm."

"Are there any more?" Judy asked. "Can I have one, mama?"

"Your dad wouldn't refuse anything from this farm. We've been promising you a kitty; maybe you should take one," Fran suggested.

"Them's too wittwe to go," Sadie warned. "Wose had some Mista James is giving away wight now."

"Ginny should know if any of those kittens are left," Bess suggested. "Where is Ginny? She should see this."

"She's making a video over there. That's true love. She's seeing it on a screen so her man can see it later on," Fran declared.

Bess spotted Ginny holding an iPad scanning it from one team to another to record the event.

"Here comes James' team," Fran announced. "He always gets the most out of his men. Listen as they make it up the hill. He's encouraging, counting, and still holding up his end of the work. He's as tough as they come," Fran added. "My husband is leading the team next to him. He's like James. He can inspire anyone to do the impossible. It's a gift. Sometimes it makes me furious because he has me pushing myself too. I do love that man of mine," Fran admitted. "Look at him."

Bess never saw Fran's husband. Her one-track mind was stuck on James. He fascinated her; everything about him was intriguing. In a calm voice he cadenced "heave men, heave men, heave men." At his prompt, the men moved the pole up the hill, their feet keeping pace with his words. The sound of his voice, accompanied with the men's grunts, seemed like a sexual chant.

The sweat was pouring down James's rugged face, his wet hair darker than the usual light brown. The bulging muscle from his elbow to his shoulder formed two huge masses on each arm, making him look more body builder than painter or shepherd. His damp tee shirt stuck to his chest, revealing the 'divine proportions' of his broad torso.

Realizing she was lusting after him, Bess blushed. Her eyes moved to find Ginny. She was sitting down now, talking on a cell phone with tears in her eyes.

"Is Ginny all right?" Bess asked Fran.

"Poor thing," Fran said. "She must be talking to Mike. She misses him so much."

"Whose Mike?" Bess asked, disoriented.

"He's her fiancé. He's still in the Army, comes home from Afghanistan in two weeks. He's the last one in the original platoon to get out of active service. In April they get married right here on The Funny Farm. We all can't wait," Fran explained.

"I thought Ginny was married to James. They have the same last name," Bess said, the shock showing on her face.

"James isn't married; Ginny is his sister," Fran explained. "Remind me. How long have you known James?"

Bess blushed and shrugged, "Only met him yesterday."

"And he invited you here?" Fran said nudging her.

"To see the kittens," Bess said, panic rising.

"Relax," Fran advised. "I'm just kidding you."

"Mista James is gonna paint my mama," Sadie said proudly. "So we have to come back."

Bess studied James and her heartbeat quickened. She felt her first surge of sexual desire in two years. Bess blushed just as James turned and saw her. He winked, despite the heavy load, the cadence, or the crowd. In that fleeting moment, he made it crystal clear why she'd been invited to The Funny Farm.

Fran leaned over and whispered, "I never knew James to paint anything but animals and scenery. You must inspire him," Fran said, nudging her again.

Rascal had been studying the mass of men moving up toward his Sadie. The baby donkey was not amused and the fact that they were carrying something that could hurt her made him furious. Sadie had knelt down and was holding him, her arms around his fuzzy neck. "It's aww wight, Wascal. I'm with you," Sadie whispered into one of his huge ears.

The little girl didn't realize that Rascal was bred from guard donkeys. He wasn't afraid of anything because he believed himself invincible. He was doing what came naturally, guarding his chosen human. He started with grumbles. As they inched too close, he threw back his head and showed his teeth. Bess looked down and spotted the problem.

"Sadie," Bess warned, "Rascal is trying to get them away. She sat down next to Sadie and helped her hold him. His little head jerked back, his teeth became exposed and Rascal began making a horrific, yodeling sound. The eeeee ooorrr comic warnings made the crowd laugh.

Bess held on as Rascal moved into full voice, now sounding like a rusty hinge opening and closing with each step the men took. The noise competed with the sound of their own leaders. The distraction made their job more difficult, their load heavier.

The crowd sensed the danger and quieted, but Rascal's protest grew louder until James' voice boomed orders and took command of all five teams, "Dig down men. Everyone stay with me."

"We all go together," the other forty-nine men called back.

"Heave men," James began anew. "Heave men, heave men." Suddenly all the poles moved in unison, the men yelling, "Yes sir" between his orders. Even Rascal shut his mouth as if the donkey understood James' demand. As each team reached the crest of the hill, they remained shouldering their load, their feet stamping in place with their comrades. Not until all the poles had completed the trip, did James order, "On my command, prepare to step apart and drop. Step apart!"

"Yes sir," rang out.

"Drop," James ordered.

"Yes sir," they answered and the noise was in perfect unison, the trees dropping together with one huge thump. The ground vibrated under everyone's feet.

"Best hill climb ever," James announced. "Together—"

"We overcome," they answered, as family members ran to celebrate their victory.

Bess stood absorbed by the scene, but Sadie ran toward James, Rascal following in pursuit. Other families embraced, despite their soldier's sweat or exhaustion. Then Bess watched James grin as Sadie jumped into his arms. He twirled her around laughing as she chatted to him, no doubt apologizing for Rascal's bellows. He patted her back gently and gazed lovingly over her little shoulder at Bess.

Primal, raw panic shook Bess to the core. Her protective motherly instinct emerged. Unlike Rascal, however, she didn't need to show her teeth or verbalize her fear. James saw it in the glare of Bess's eyes, the grinding of her teeth, her fists balled up in fury. He knew he had crossed some invisible line that frightened Bess.

James lowered Sadie to the ground and suggested she go congratulate Judy's father. James watched as Bess' eyes followed Sadie as she went. He saw some tension release when the other man lifted Sadie and threw her up in the air. Bess studied Sadie as she ran off holding hands with Judy, joining the other children and families as they ran down the hill. He could see her reasoning that perhaps Sadie was not focused on only James. He turned before she looked his way, his back to her as he talked to the other men and lifted some of their children to celebrate.

Bess studied James, thinking, *Maybe I'm too protective. I'm not used to sharing Sadie with anyone. It was only the two of us for so very long, but we don't belong here. I can't let Sadie get all caught up in this place. This isn't real life. It's like a dream world, where a donkey loves only her and her red-haired, girl cat is being nurtured. Where goat milk can be had whenever you milk Dipsy. This is like falling down a hole into a fantasy life. We've got to get out of here.*

James turned in time to see Bess running down the hill to catch Sadie. He knew she would leave as soon as she found her. He knew he had to let her go if he ever expected them to return again.

Bess pretended to smile as she caught up to Sadie. James watched as they talked to Fran, Judy, and her dad. Then Bess turned and briefly waved goodbye to James. He forced a smile on his face and waved a casual goodbye.

His eyes watched them as they walked toward the little barn, Bess' red hair shining like fire, Sadie's blonde head bobbing as she walked. He knew they would settle Rascal back into his stall and stay awhile to hold their kittens. They would stay only if he didn't join them. He let them be even though he already missed them both. He knew he had overwhelmed them.

James shook his head, reasoning that all the characteristics needed for commanding a platoon were probably not appealing to a woman. Bess wouldn't be interested in anyone who demanded so much from his men. *I don't know squat about women,*" he realized.

James found himself looking for Ginny. He needed her advice, tutelage, and insight. His sister would have to teach him how to court Bess. She had to; he had already realized how much Bess and Sadie would enrich his lonely life.

James watched as their car drove away from the farm. Only then did he walk back to the little barn. Rascal was settled down, so exhausted that he only lifted his head once before falling back to sleep. James sat down and lifted Bess' kitten. He nuzzled the calico cat against his nose, searching for her scent. He smelled her perfume, faint but still there. He closed his eyes and pictured her holding Callie. When he opened them, he saw a note, pinned to the wall over the kittens.

James stood up and yanked it off the wall. He lowered the kitten gently onto the straw so she could get back to Rose.

James walked over and sat on a bale of hay. The note said:

James-

Thank you for all you have done for our kittens. We truly appreciate it. Hope Rascal isn't spoiled by his day with Sadie. We both had a wonderful time.

I need to warn you. While in the field with your sheep, I noticed several of them are going to give birth in the next few days. Fran told me that you bred for April births due to the bears. I think your Ram found a way into the meadow and impregnated about ten of your sheep. Since the mother will break from their herd mentality when they are going to give birth, the bears may find the sheep and her lambs easy targets. I'm afraid they may be injured or killed.

I've marked the ones I'm worried about by tying some of my yarn around their necks. Red means due very soon, blue means in a week. There may be more I missed. I ran out of time.

Good luck,

Bess

James rubbed his head with his hand realizing that Bess was a real shepherd. He wasn't. He was just trying to keep their platoon's dream alive. He still believed that without that crazy dream none of them would have survived the heat, exhaustion, despair, and reoccurring attacks from the enemy.

James's best friend and second in command had been Mitchell. He'd been a shepherd before 9/11 and shortly after he joined the army. In the sandy outpost in the mountains of Afghanistan, Mitchell had dreamed up The Funny Farm. He had used the dream of the sheep farm like a shepherd's hook to pull them out of despair and take their minds off the bullets that whizzed by their heads. When they hadn't the strength to dream of anything else, he held classes on shearing, feeding, and raising sheep. The Funny Farm was named and organized right down to each month's activity. It was like a video game that they all played together. It had held their attention when the real world seemed too much to bear.

James shook his head as he remembered a particular fierce firefight. Hal was wounded, bleeding out. He'd been a lumberjack in Oregon. That night, while they held back the enemy and hoped for a copter to get Hal out, he'd helped them plan March's activity. He'd told them all the things lumberjacks did to compete. This month had been for Hal. And every one of the men knew it.

Now The Funny Farm was a reality, but Mitchell, the real shepherd, was among the fallen. James was just trying to do the best he could to keep their dream alive, but he was shooting from the hip.

Hell, James thought, *I don't know what I'm doing on this farm. I don't even know how to be a damn civilian. I'm just a painter. I should've checked the sheep over. Mitchell should have lived. He would have known about all this shit,* James decided.

He placed his head in his hands and cried, reliving the day he had marched his best friend into battle. He could still feel his warm blood dripping through his fingers into the hot sand, as he had carried him all the way back to the God forsaken outpost in that hell hole of a desert.

Seven

"I'm mad at you," Sadie said as she pouted in the back seat, her arms crossed on her chest.

"I don't know why," Bess said, in an innocent tone.

"Cause you took me fwom my teachea, Judy," Sadie said whipping a tear away. "I want to go back."

"But we were only invited to see the kittens. We don't belong to that group. It's not our party," Bess explained. "Everyone did like you. You were a real hit." She looked in the rearview mirror and noticed a small smile appear on her daughter's lips.

"Wascal wuuvs me, so does James," Bess suggested.

Bess calmed herself, taking in a deep breath of fresh air. "He likes you, everyone did. You are a very nice girl. What do you think the word love means?" Bess asked.

"When you weawwy, weawwy like em," Sadie answered, after thinking.

"Do you love ice cream?"

"Yup, suwe do," Sadie answered.

"So do I. I eat it all the time and I know it will taste the same all the time. Do you love Millie?"

"I do wuuv hew so much. She's my baby now," Sadie said, hugging herself in lieu of her kitten.

"I love her too. She's part of our family, so is my Callie. We love our family best of all," Bess explained. "We also love God. He is part of us and our family. We can also love very good friends, like Singing Bird."

"I wuuvs her very much," Sadie admitted.

"We can like people but we only love a very few people who feel just like members of our family," Bess added.

Bess watched as Sadie thought about what she had said. Bess added, "Rascal will always live at The Funny Farm. You can like him very, very much but you won't love him as much as Millie 'cause he won't be part of your family. You might not even see him again after we take our kittens home. I want you to remember that. It doesn't mean that you can't have fun with him; it means you know it's only for a little while."

"I weally, weally like Wascal, Mama," Sadie admitted.

"So do I. I will look forward to seeing him when we go to pick up the kittens."

"I weally like Mista James," Sadie added. "He weally likes you."

"I think he likes everyone," Bess said quickly.

"No, not like you," Sadie added. "Him wants to paint you," Sadie added after thinking about it for a while.

Bess answered quickly, "I'll be too busy playing with you to sit real still while he paints me."

"What color does he want to paint you?" Sadie asked.

Bess laughed and shrugged. "I don't want to find out. I like the color I am now. Let's eat out tonight. Where do you want to go?"

"McDonalds," Sadie shouted and everything else was forgotten.

Ginny heard Shep barking happily as James climbed down the steps from his tree house studio. He'd slept there ever since the party had broken up. She greeted him at the front porch with a cup of coffee. "I saw you looking out at the field with your binoculars. Did everything look good?" Ginny asked.

"So far, so good," James answered, as he nodded good morning. He stooped down and patted Shep. "So you're home again. How was your date? Are the Brewsters gonna have any puppies?" he asked laughing. James stood up and looked at his sister. "Is that coffee for me? I could sure drink a cup. I'm going for a walk through the field and check the sheep."

"I thought so; that's why it's in this paper cup. I'm coming with you though; you've avoided me for the past few days, and I think we need to talk," Ginny said, falling in step with her brother.

"I don't need to talk. I've decided that things are best left the way they are," James said, sipping as he walked.

"Bull shit," Ginny said, keeping her eyes looking in front.

"Don't start with me, little sis," James said smiling. "Who taught you to talk that way anyhow?"

"You did," Ginny said shrugging. "Listen James. I've been thinking about this. I'm going to make you an offer. You listen to everything I have to say, and then I'll never bring the subject up again."

"Like the thing they say about Las Vegas, except now it's— What happens in the sheep pasture stays in the sheep pasture?" James said laughing.

"Yes, that works for me," Ginny said, punching him in the arm.

"I think I raised you to be too much like a guy," James worried. "Thank God Mike likes you that way."

"Good place to start," Ginny said as they walked. "Mike loves me even though you raised me to be a tom boy. He doesn't care. Did you know that at first he thought I was strange. A real nut case?" Ginny added.

"He did?"

"Yes. Told me I scared him. I was too honest and too transparent. He could see how I felt about him before he even knew my name," Ginny said smiling.

"I can see that," James said, pushing her lightly as they walked.

"We are too much alike," Ginny admitted. "I can see how you feel about Bess. You've already decided you love her, haven't you?"

"I'm not good for her," James said. "She's been through something real hard. I don't know what, but she's better off without getting tied up with me. I haven't the slightest idea how to deal with women. I couldn't help her or Sadie."

"Chicken shit," Ginny said with a laugh.

"You really have to watch that mouth of yours," James said, shaking his head.

"You really have to stop playing the martyr," Ginny protested. "The only thing you ever wanted is that studio you built in that tree. You never wanted all this," she added, sweeping her hand over the meadows and all the livestock. "You're doing this to keep a promise made to your platoon."

"I kinda like it now. I just don't think I'm too good at it," James admitted. "I like the sheep and goats. That donkey's gonna help a lot when he grows up. I like painting my own animals. I'd miss them if they weren't here."

"The farm has been good for you. I see that. Its let your softer side come out," Ginny said, touching his arm gently. "The farm will be lonely once Mike and I get married. I'll be far away in Wisconsin. I want you to be happy too."

"I messed up royally with Bess. Came on too strong. I can't imagine what she thought of me being all tough guy, Commander. Probably thinks I'm a dumb ass, control freak," James said.

"You are a tough guy, dumb ass, control freak," Ginny explained, but only because you end up in charge. You were always the Captain, President, or leader of any group. Why was that?"

"I have no idea. I guess I like to be in charge," James admitted.

"I think it's time for you to stop all that in-charge crap. You need help, brother. For once in your life admit it?" Ginny suggested

"What do you mean?" James asked as they both walked through the gate into the pasture.

"Tell Bess the truth. Tell her you need help on this farm. You need her to tell you what you're doing wrong and start by asking her how to get that gross goat milk to taste good. No one can stand that stuff. It's awful. We can't even give it away," Ginny said laughing.

"She'll think I'm pathetic," James answered.

"Not if you tell her how The Funny Farm came about. While you're at it, tell her that you haven't a clue how to talk to a woman," Ginny added.

"You make me sound like a caveman," James said shaking his head.

"Well?" Ginny said shrugging and looking over at him. "You sort of are."

"She's going to be afraid to come near this farm after the last time," James said shaking his head.

"Apologize if you came on too strong with both her and Sadie," Ginny advised. "If my kid had been through all she has, I'd be careful who got close to her. The kid just started talking. She's still fragile. One ass who says the wrong thing or disappoints her, and she could stop talking forever."

"I never looked at it that way," James said.

"Of course you didn't," Ginny explained. "You're a caveman who just got back to the real world. You need help, Bro."

"Why would she want to help me?" James asked.

"She won't quite yet," Ginny said with a smile, "but Fran and I are signed up for a spinning class with Bess. She will in a few days. I promise you that. We have your back," Ginny said, pushing her brother as they walked through the field.

"I don't want her to feel uncomfortable in her new home. You better let her be," James suggested.

"I like her. So does Fran. I'm really intrigued with learning to spin. I think it'll be a real surprise to Mike. I can do it in Wisconsin when we move. It'll be a cool hobby, something different. You can send me all the fleece I need. Fran and I want to learn how to do it," Ginny explained.

"Just what intrigued you about spinning?" James asked, suspicious.

"You didn't see her when she spins," Ginny explained. "You were out playing soldier, cutting down trees with your platoon. "It's almost like magic. She took some of your fleece that she'd washed before she got here. It was combed out into roving. Then she sat there, in the meadow, and she'd grab a piece of the roving and start peddling her wheel and soon it was going onto the wheel and turning into yarn. It was so great."

"Sis," James exclaimed, "you really do like her."

"I do," Ginny admitted. "I like her kid too. She's so cute and that little donkey is nuts over Sadie. You have good taste, James. They're worth fighting for. Don't you dare chicken out."

"If a man starts out being honest about all he doesn't know," James asked, "how can a woman ever respect him?"

"If a man can't be honest with a woman," Ginny explained, "then she'll never respect him. Women know that being honest takes more courage than being strong or in charge."

"What can I offer her?" James asked.

Ginny looked around and laughed, saying, "Why don't you start out with 200 sheep?"

James reached out and patted the heads of his sheep as they circled around them. "They could win anyone's heart," he admitted. "Right girls?" Three baaed in reply. James turned toward Ginny suggesting, "Don't come on too strong, like I did."

"I'm no caveman. Fran and I know just what we're doing. We don't plan to talk about you or this farm," Ginny said laughing.

"Really?"

"It will drive her crazy. Anyone who marks the pregnant sheep with different colored yarn is someone who truly cares. She's dying to know how they are doing, if they had their babies, how many they had," Ginny said with a smile.

"She'll just ask you," James warned. "She's from Montana. They don't play games or beat around the bush. I was stationed with a man from Montana."

"Fran and I will know nothing, except that you have your hands full with too much and that you really have no clue what to do," Ginny added.

"I don't think she cares that much," James said, discouraged.

"Fran saw Bess' face as she watched you command your men. She liked it; you had her blushing. That was until she found out you were single. Then she got really scared. She ran because she was afraid of how you were feeling about her and how she was feeling about you. You're both afraid of being hurt. You've been beat up by the world and afraid to try again."

"Really?" James asked. "She was looking at me?"

"No, James," Ginny said laughing. "Fran said she was drooling over you."

Eight

Bess rolled over in bed and stretched. She had another good night's sleep, undisturbed by the usual nightmares. She smiled; it felt good to wake up rested and happy. She closed her eyes, eager to retreat back to her dream, until she realized the fantasy she was trying to recreate. Her eyes shot open and she questioned, *What am I doing?*

Bess sat up, letting her shoulders droop. She looked over at the picture on her bureau and sighed. In the photo, little Sadie was in her arms, smiling with her two front teeth missing, and Drew, her husband, was grinning. Bess got out of bed and walked over to the picture, picking it up, and taking it with her to the window. She lifted the shade and studied it closely in the bright sunlight that now poured in.

Drew had his arm around her shoulder, like he always had. Bess smiled as she touched his face. She couldn't remember much of her life when Drew didn't have his arm around her shoulder. They'd been best friends from the time she was six. "Sadie's age!" Bess whispered as she tilted her head and remembered back.

They'd chased each other up and down trees, hills and valleys. They'd started their first day of school together and every year thereafter. She remembered her high school graduation. Drew had gotten down on one knee, right there in front of all thirty members of their class and proposed just before she went up on stage to get her diploma.

"Drew," Bess whispered as she moved back to sit on the bed. "I can't believe you're gone." The light changed and suddenly Bess noticed the dust on the picture frame. "Has it been that long?" she asked, as she carefully wiped it clean.

"What ya doing Mommy?" Sadie asked as she walked into her bedroom.

"I'm looking at this picture," Bess said, raising one arm to invite Sadie over. "Look, you're missing your front teeth."

"I wook siwwe in that pictuwe," Sadie decided. "I'm all gwown up now. When can I go see my Miwwie? I was dweaming about my kitty and Wascal."

"Don't you want to look at the picture with me?" Bess asked, "and give me a hug?"

"I saw it wots and wots of time. Mama, can I take a pictua of Miwwie, Cawwie, and Wose. I want one of Wascal too. I'm gonna bwing it to schoow and show the kids," Sadie announced.

"You'd have to tell them all about The Funny Farm," Bess said, walking to put the picture frame back on her dresser. "Would you do that?"

"I'm weady, Mommy. I know just what to say. Wisten. I'm going to tawk duwing Show and Teww."

Sadie struck a pose at the foot of the bed, her little hands holding a pretend picture. "I just stawted tawking again. Yous have to hewp me 'cause I need pwactice. This is a pictuwe of my kitty Miwwie. She's the wed-haiwed kitty. This is my fwiend donkey, Wascal. He onwe wikes me. He fowwos me evewywhere when we go to Mista James' fawm." Sadie stopped and looked at her mother, beaming proudly.

The teacher will wonder who Mr. James is," Bess thought. She looked away, surprised by her own reaction. *Why do I care about that? I should just be glad Sadie's ready to start talking.*

"It was bad? " Sadie asked. "I did bad?"

"No, honey. It was perfect just the way you said it. I'm happy you're going to talk at school. I'm so proud of you," Bess said, as she walked over and hugged her daughter.

"Can we take pictuwes today afta schoow?" Sadie asked growing excited. "We can take them to the stowe and they can make the pictuwes in one houwa," Sadie suggested. She lifted her one finger and Bess noticed the nail wasn't bleeding.

"Have you stopped biting your nails?" Bess asked stunned.

"Yup," Sadie answered. "Judy said I'll get wowms if I bite them. If I stop, Judy's gonna paint them pink."

Bess reached down and lifted Sadie into her arms. She turned to look at their reflection in the bureau mirror, then compared it to the photo. Sadie was so much bigger, so grown up. *It's time to move on,* Bess realized. *Trudy's right. Spring is here, and it's time to move on.*

"I'm not sure about the worms, but I would love to see your fingernails painted pink. I might even buy you polish of your own," Bess admitted. "I think this is a very good day to take pictures. I teach spinning class to Miss Ginny and Miss Fran. I'll ask them if Judy would like to meet us at the farm so she can meet your kitty, and we can take pictures."

Sadie kissed her mom's cheek and wiggled out of her arms. "Good, and I want to take a picture of Judy and me, and one of Mista James," Sadie said, as she ran down the hall to get dressed.

I'd like a picture of Mr. James, Bess realized.

Trudy greeted Ginny as she arrived asking, "Are you James Turner's sister?"

"I am," Ginny answered, a look of concern on her face. "Did he call here? Does my cell phone work here?"

"Yes, it'll work here," Bess said, reassuring her. "Are you worried about him reaching you?"

"Yes," Ginny answered hesitating. "He's got his hands full today. Seems four or more sheep are lambing. I almost didn't come. I wouldn't know what to do anyway. He told me to go and promised to call if he got in trouble."

"Do you want to call him from our phone?" Trudy suggested, concern written all over her face.

"No," Ginny said, shrugging. "As long as he can reach me here. I think he has your office number too."

Trudy admitted, "I knew you were James' sister as soon as you came in. You're as good looking as your brother."

"Thanks, I guess," Ginny said smiling.

"How come your brother is still single? He's the best looking man any of us has ever seen," Trudy continued.

"I tease him that he's a caveman when it comes to women," Ginny explained. "In truth, he was over in Afghanistan on and off for years on end. His platoon was either driving terrorists out of the mountain caves or holding onto remote outposts. When he was home on leave, he never dated much. Said it wasn't fair to get involved because of what he was going back to. Some of his men didn't come home."

"Well, he's home now," Trudy said. "I bet there's a line of women calling him up."

"No, not really. He's not a flirt. Probably doesn't even make eye contact with any women," Ginny suggested. "I leave for Wisconsin after I get married. I sure hope he finds someone after I leave. That farm will be too much for him to handle all alone. I think it's too much already. He's got so many sheep now."

"When did lambing begin?" Trudy asked.

"Yesterday," Ginny answered. "He'll be fine. He made it through last year."

"But how long has he had his sheep?" Bess asked, growing concerned.

"This is the third year, why?" Fran asked.

"He has all Bluefaced Leicester sheep. They have one or two babies the first two years. After that, the flock will reproduce itself by two hundred and fifty percent" Bess explained.

"What does that mean?" Ginny asked.

"I mean, once they reach the age of three, most Bluefaced Leicester sheep will have three, sometimes even four lambs. They're among the most prolific of all breeds. The births get complicated. Ewes may need some help," Bess said taking off her apron.

"You're kidding me, right?" Ginny asked.

"No, I'm dead serious. Doesn't James know all this?"

"No, he doesn't. He has no idea what he's in for," Ginny said as she reached for her phone. They all stood around and waited for James to pick up.

"I can't talk now," James yelled. "Got my hands full." The connection broke and Ginny looked over at Bess announcing, "He hung up, said he's got his hands full."

Bess turned to Carol, the owner of The Mannings and said, "I think I better get over there and see if he needs help. I've saved many a lamb in trouble over the years. I know every trick in the book."

"You go," Carol said, "if it's all right with Fran and Ginny, you can hold their class another day."

"Yes, please go help him. Stay as long as you're needed. I can pick Sadie up at the bus and take her over to our house," Fran suggested. "Where does she get off the bus?"

"Sadie's bus drops her off at the end of this street. The driver knows me. I'll get her off the bus," Trudy suggested. "Sadie will be here at the shop waiting for you, Fran. Come after you get your little girl."

"I've got to go home and grab my things," Bess said. "Does James have birthing lubricant?"

"I don't know. Should I stop at the feed store and get some. Should I pick up anything else?" Ginny asked.

Bess grabbed a piece of paper and wrote as she talked. "Yes, get a package of lambing rope. Buy three while you're there and disinfectant and lubricant. Get four jugs of lubricant," Bess said shoving the list toward Ginny. "I'll need some water in a bucket. Make it half full and bring the rest of the supplies out to the field."

"Come quickly, please," Ginny asked. "I'm not much help when it comes to lambing."

"You can bring the lambs and their mothers to the barn. It's too early. The bears are still hungry," Bess shouted. "No one mention bears to Sadie. Please, no one say the word bear around her," she shouted before running to her car.

James had four ewes lambing at the same time. He wasn't concerned until he noticed what a hard time they were having. Then one ewe finally delivered three lambs and James knew he was over his head in trouble.

James waited for an hour and then carried two of the lambs toward the little barn; the mother stayed behind with the third one. He ran back to the field to retrieve the last lamb and their mother when he heard the cry of a ewe in pain.

A chill went through his body as he got a premonition of what may lay ahead. His cell phone rang again as he was running toward the troubled ewe. "I still can't talk, Ginny," James said as he ran.

"I know. Bess is coming and I'm getting supplies. She says that since the flock is three years old, they might have three lambs and some trouble giving birth."

"How long before she gets here?" James asked. "I've got a ewe in real trouble."

"Not long. I'm at the feed store getting lambing rope, disinfectant and lubricant," Ginny answered.

"What the hell is that for?" James asked.

"Bess knows. Says she knows about every trick in the book to help save lambs," Ginny answered.

"Thank God," James said before hanging up.

The ewe couldn't deliver; she was in pain and one lamb's head was already out, the rest stuck in the birth canal. James had been stroking the little lamb's head, happy to see it was at least breathing. He felt lost, frantic, and desperate to save it. Then he looked up and saw Bess. She was running toward him, her boots slowing her progress. In one hand she held a large, wooden shepherd's hook and the sight took his breath away. He stared at the hook, a lump in his throat. *I'll be damned,* James thought. *Just like the one Mitchell made from that stick in Afghanistan.*

"How are you doing?" Bess asked upon seeing the expression on James' face.

"Not well at all," James admitted. "I've got a lamb with its head out and she's stuck."

"I need the lubricant, lambing rope, and a bucket. Did Ginny bring them out to the field?" Bess asked.

"Right here," Ginny said, as she joined them. "What can I do to help?"

"Ask James," Bess said, as she knelt behind the sheep.

"I'm lost," James admitted. "They always delivered without any problems before.

"You only had half as many sheep last year," Bess reminded him. "If I get involved, they'll be times you'll have to follow my instructions. Is that all right?" Bess asked as she took the bucket and poured disinfectant into the water in the bucket. "I can't do this alone. I'll need your help, but just do as I say."

"You've got my undivided attention," James said. "I'm just glad you're here."

"Ginny, I need you to keep an eye on the other ewes who have separated from the flock. Take Shep with you. Big, Bad Bertha and Rascal will take care of the rest. The guard animals sense what's going on," Bess advised.

"James, I need you to turn this ewe upside down. I'll help." With Bess using the shepherd's hook, they both turned the ewe upside down, the little lamb's head still protruding from the ewe.

After disinfecting her hands, Bess poured some lubricant over the lamb's head. "I'm tying some of the lambing robe around this little one's head, making sure I put the rope around her head but not around her neck. I put the last part running between her jaws, see. Now I won't strangle her when I pull on it." Bess said to James.

"Yes, I see that. Now what?" James asked.

"Now I'm going to put my hands inside and check for the feet. I think they're in the wrong position, and the lamb can't slide out. Yup, they're bent over and won't make it through," Bess explained.

"What do we do to help?" James asked again.

"I'm going to reinsert the lamb's head back into the ewe. I can't reposition it until I push the lamb back through the birth canal. I have to get it back into the womb," Bess said.

"You're kidding, right?" James said.

"Not at all," Bess urged. "Now watch me. I put lubricant on the head and the ears and push gently on the lamb's head. I have small hands so this is easier for me. You'd have a bit more trouble. Never push too hard. Remember the ewe is pushing against you."

"Will I have to do this?" James asked.

"Chances are you will. Your flock is three years old. Bluefaced Leicester can have three, even four, lambs after three years," Bess said. "There you go, little one, back in your mom. Now let me turn you. Yup, here they are, bent over."

"James, please hand me another section of lambing rope. I'm going to tie one on the leg as I ease it through. I can't find the other leg yet," Bess announced.

One little hoof emerged in Bess's hand. "Now watch, James. I have to tie the lambing rope between the hoof and the knee–right here in this narrow section of her leg. If you tie it over the hoof, it might break her leg. If you tie it too high, it will pull out the knee. Just carefully, like this," Bess said, slipping the knot on. "Where is that second leg, Mamma? I'm going to find it and help you out," Bess said.

"The lamb was breathing before. Is it suffocating now?" James asked.

"No, but good questions. The lamb should still have the umbilical cord connected, so it's all right. We should hurry though, in case it broke it when I pushed her back in."

"Here's the other leg. Now I take that out and put the loop over it like the other. Now we need to see that little head again. I'll pull ever so gently," Bess said and the head re-emerged from the mother.

"Now James," Bess urged, "let's get mama on her side," Bess instructed. The lamb slid out and Bess massaged it until it began breathing. "There we go," She announced. We don't want to cut the umbilical cord. It's better if it breaks off naturally as she separates from her Mamma. We want the blood to flow into the lamb for a bit yet. Okay, now let's get her up where her mom can see her," Bess suggested.

James moved the lamb and rubbed her gently. "She's breathing," James announced.

"Good thing, because her sibling is on the way. Let's see if this one comes naturally. Two feet emerged and within minutes, number two lamb emerged. James and Bess smiled at each other.

"Is that it? Is she done lambing?" James asked.

Bess was up palpating the ewe's stomach. "Nope. One is left. I better see if the legs are in the wrong position. It could have happened when I pushed the first lamb in."

Bess slipped her hand in and checked around. "Yes, same problem as the first one. We have to repeat what we did, but it should be easier because this head is still inside," Bess decided.

"Ten minutes later Bess and James sat next to each other, exhausted but happy. They watched as the three lambs were checked over by their mother.

Bess reached over and took James' hand. "We did it," she whispered. "We make a good team."

Nine

"We could make a great team," James said as he lightly squeezed her hand.

"I've never held hands with any man but my husband," Bess said shyly. "I met him when I was six, Sadie's age."

"Really?" James asked.

"Drew was the son of my dad's best friend. We lived in Dupuyer, a small town in Montana. I'm sure you've never heard of it," Bess said.

"I think I did. It's around Glacier Park, isn't it?" James asked.

"Yes, how do you know that?" Bess exclaimed, as she slowly took her hand away.

"A few men in my platoon were from Montana," James paused and looked out over the field. "One was from around there. He was my best friend," James added.

A solemn quiet fell upon the meadow, a quiet they both knew he needed. Bess finally broke through, saying, "Did you know that Montana has the third lowest population density in the United States? There are only 6.58 people for every square mile in Montana." She turned to look at James adding, "If he had anything to do with sheep, I'd have met your friend."

They both sat watching the mother feed her new lambs, while Rascal brayed at a sheep who'd gone too far from the flock. Big, Bad Bertha stayed close to the little donkey as if she was training Rascal. Shep was beside Ginny, helping her keep watch over the lambing ewes in the far corners. Finally, James said, "He was a shepherd. He should have been the one to live, not me. Mitchell would have known what to do today."

Bess let the March wind blow his words away. Only then did she turn and say, "I knew a Mitchell. If it was the same man, I don't think he'd question why it was him who died."

James smiled and shook his head before deciding, "You're right. He'd call me a dumb ass for thinking about it so much."

"Must have been the same guy," Bess said, nodding her head in silent agreement. "He was eight years older than Drew and I, had his own 4-H Sheep Club. We met him at the 4-H regional camp, I must've been around twelve." Bess moved over toward the lambs and repositioned the smallest, making sure it was sucking properly.

When she returned, she sat beside James and added, "Mitchell was in charge of the *sheep kids*. That's what they called us at camp. We were so proud of that name, probably because it meant we were Mitchell's kids. All the girls had crushes on him. He was tall, dark, handsome, and twenty. He taught us so much that week," Bess said smiling sadly. "He told us he was going to enlist in the Army."

"I can picture him walking around with a bunch of teenagers following him. He'd have liked that," James added. "I'm the same age as Mitchell; he'd have been thirty-eight this March." He turned adding, "Do you mind hanging out with a guy that old?"

"I'm thirty now and sometimes I feel even older," Bess said shrugging. "Life can do that to you; besides I've got a kid. Some men don't like hanging out with a woman who has a kid?"

"I think Sadie's the icing on your cake." They both laughed and a comfortable quiet refreshed James' thoughts.

"Mitchell's how I ended up with The Funny Farm," James explained. "It sure is a small world, isn't it?" Bess just nodded. "We were hanging onto a small outpost in the southernmost region of Afghanistan. We were all tired and on edge. The Taliban came at us like cowards in the dark, placing IED's wherever they thought we'd patrol. They'd also plant homemade rockets at night, then go home and wait. You never knew when the rockets would go off or how powerful they'd be. They'd set them off with cell phones or kitchen timers."

James raked his hands through his hair and added, "One day, we lost three of our men to those asses. You don't need to hear this."

"I do," Bess insisted. "I think we've both experienced things that most haven't."

James smiled and said, "I think we might have. It probably does me good to talk about it, but I don't tell anyone this crap. Most don't really want to hear."

"It's only me, you, and the sheep. If it helps you to talk, I'd like to hear," Bess suggested.

"We were sitting there in our outpost watching for their next sneak attack. All of a sudden, a flock of sheep show up, walking not more than three kilometers away with one shepherd. Some men wanted to fire, saying the shepherd was holding a rocket launcher. You see all kinds of things when you're looking for it," James explained.

"I can understand," Bess agreed.

James continued remembering, "Mitchell yelled, *Stand down! That's just the shepherd's hook. He uses it to keep his sheep safe, you assholes. The shepherd and his sheep get safe passage, or I'll beat the living crap out of you.*"

James looked over at Bess and added, "That was the beginning of The Funny Farm. The rest of our stay out in that hellhole, Mitchell taught all of us about sheep; and he and I made a pact to buy this farm. The guys promised to come whenever they could on the last Saturday of each month. They spent more time talking about what activity they'd do each month than Mitchell and me. We talked about the farm."

"You named it The Funny Farm because?" Bess asked.

"Because we all decided if we didn't have a place to get together after what we'd been through, we'd all end up in The Funny Farm. You know, in some hospital for PTSD, Post Traumatic Stress Disorder." James admitted.

"Like your flashback?" Bess asked.

James looked away towards the forest and shook his head, admitting, "Like that."

"I guess that's what makes us alike. Both Sadie and I have been diagnosed with PTSD," Bess admitted. "We have flashbacks too."

"I gathered that," James explained. "It must have been terrible when Drew died."

"It was terrible, and the way he died was worse," Bess said, waving her hand as if to signal the topic was not open for discussion.

"So how did you pick Pennsylvania?" James asked.

"I saw an ad in a fiber magazine. The Mannings sounded like the answer to our prayers. Pennsylvania was different, not so cold, and lots of new people who don't pity us. We needed to get where no one knew us," Bess shared.

"Do you like it?" James asked.

"I do and Sadie really likes it now that she's met new friends," Bess said. "But I'm afraid to let her get too close to you."

"Why, Bess? I'd never do anything to hurt Sadie," James urged.

"I sense that about you. That's another reason I'm drawn to you, but she's had enough losses in her life," Bess said.

"You're drawn to me?" James asked.

Bess turned to look at the man. She shrugged and suggested, "I think we're both drawn to each other. Am I right?"

"Yes, I'm falling hard for you," James admitted.

"It's the disinfectant, very sexy stuff," Bess said laughing. "You're not falling for me; you just like being around someone with so much in common."

"You mean the flashbacks?" James asked

"No, I mean all these sheep," Bess said, waving her hand toward the grazing flock. "Don't fall for me," Bess insisted. "I'm not available. I need to focus on only Sadie right now."

"Only one thing at a time," James said nodding his head. "Sadie told me you handle one thing at a time."

"I focus on one thing at a time," Bess said smiling, "but I can handle much more than that. I could sure use some companionship now and then." He watched as she lifted one of her eyebrows and tilted her head.

"I'm probably not good company," James warned. "I've never spent much time with women, dating, and all that stuff."

"Then that makes two of us. Drew and I grew up together, never really dated. I've never experienced being around a stranger. Getting to know him and all that."

"All that?" James said looking over at her.

"I saw you trudging up the hill with that log on your shoulder. I've never felt butterflies like that," Bess admitted. "You really turned me on. I could hardly breathe," Bess admitted.

"Then why did you leave so suddenly?" James asked. "I thought I screwed it up royally with all that shouting and stomping around."

"No, James. I ran because I felt bad wanting you so much. I felt like it wasn't fair to Drew's memory and not good for Sadie."

"But you came back," James said hopefully.

"Sadie made me see that it's all right to move forward. She's sick of just looking back at old photos. She wants to take new ones on this farm," Bess explained. "So do I."

James stared at Bess, his heart pounding. "I don't want to disappoint you. I've been with women, you know, one-night stands and a few flings just before reporting back to base."

"So you've never made love, just had sex," Bess said calmly.

"Since I don't know the difference," James admitted, "I guess you're right. Do you have to be in love to make love?"

"Not by my definition. I think having sex can be like the animals we live among, fulfilling and exciting. Lord knows I could use a session like that," Bess admitted, "but there's another kind of lovemaking. I don't think you need to be in love to take time, to be tender with each other, and explore each other's bodies slowly."

"Now that I haven't done," James admitted

"I could teach you how," Bess said unashamed.

"I forgot how direct you are in Montana. Why would you?" James asked confused.

"I'm in lust of your divine proportions," Bess admitted, "and I think you're a good person. You wouldn't play head games with me."

"Well, I think you're a beautiful woman: freckles, red hair, and a passion for what and who you love," James admitted.

"Yup. I'll give you the first lesson right now," Bess suggested, "then we need to get these lambs and their mom safely in the barn."

"What? Right here in the field?" James asked growing confused.

"It requires limited physical contact," Bess urged.

"I don't know if I'm relieved or disappointed," James admitted.

Bess looked at James, his eagerness was apparent and it gave her courage. She smiled and instructed, "I want you to feel the skin on my arm." Bess pushed up the sleeve of her jacket exposing her forearm.

James rubbed his hand up her arm to her elbow. He looked at her and said, "You have soft skin. It's very pale."

"Now lift your hand and don't put any pressure on your finger tips. Just let the pads of each finger move slowly up my arm. Close your eyes while you do it," Bess instructed.

James moved closer to Bess, carefully following her bidding. He closed his eyes and felt the warmth of her skin, the tiny hairs on her arm. He moved his fingertips back to find her pulse and felt the beat of her heart increase in intensity. He experienced his first moment of true intimacy, and it aroused him beyond expectation.

James opened his eyes to find hers closed, her mouth opened ever so slightly, just enough for her to be gently biting her own bottom lip. All his insecurities vanished.

"I can't believe the difference," he admitted, as he lifted his hand and rubbed his fingertips against her cheek. Bess's eyes fluttered open. She blushed and he felt the heat rise to her face. He found it intoxicating. "What's next?" he murmured.

"I've had the craziest dreams since the last time I was on this farm. You'll laugh if I tell you," Bess said.

"Maybe with you, but I'd never laugh at you," James promised, dropping his hand from her face.

"I saw the film Titanic in a movie theatre in Conrad, Montana. It had a scene that I'll never forget," Bess said smiling. "I thought of it as you were trudging up the hill." Bess watched his reaction gauging if he was truly interested in her or only what she could do for him.

"Bess, tell me. I want to know," he urged, and she saw sincerity in his body language.

"There's a scene in the movie where these two people meet each other on the Titanic. He's an artist like you are," she said smiling. "They become friends and learn to trust each other and finally he goes to her room, and she takes off all her clothes and he sketches her," Bess said looking into his eyes. "I keep dreaming of doing that with you. Exactly like they did it. Except you would sketch me naked in your tree house," she almost whispered.

She watched as his lips parted, but nothing came out. Finally he asked, "What happens after the sketch is done?"

"Then you get to run your fingertips all over my body," Bess said, in a deep, sexual tone.

"And then?" James asked,

"You improvise," Bess suggested, lifting that perfectly curved red eyebrow.

"Help," Ginny called, breaking their mood. "We need help over here."

Ten

James rose first, extending his hand to help Bess. She accepted standing up but then she surprised him by walking forward and hugging him around his waist. James reacted by wrapping his arms gently around her, lowering his lips to her head and kissing it.

Bess felt the sensation and shivered. It had been so long since she'd felt the warmth of a man's arms, felt the thrill of a stolen kiss. She lifted her head and whispered into his ear, "To a woman, nothing is sexier than the first time a man takes you in his arms and you sense if you fit together." She looked up into his eyes and smiled. "We seem to fit perfectly."

Bess watched as he blinked, his hands gently rubbing her back. "I want to take your hand and head for that tree house," James suggested.

"We have work to do," Bess said stepping back. She took in a deep breath and looked around her, composing her own resolve. Finally she shrugged and suggested, "While you take this new family into the barn, I think I'll go help out a ewe or two."

James watched as she bent over and placed her supplies into the bucket. She stood before him, the shepherd's hook in one hand, the bucket in the other. They stared at each other in silence; then she shrugged, turned, and quickly moved toward the sheep in need.

Bess spent the afternoon monitoring the ewes that were lambing, assisting in two more births. By four o'clock, eighteen lambs and their six mothers were in the small barn.

Bess stayed in the field to palpitate the stomachs of the ewes she had previously marked with yarn. She spent another two hours checking to make sure she hadn't missed any other sheep near lambing. Finally she met up with Ginny and James announcing, "I think there will be two, possibly three, ewes lambing tonight or tomorrow. The rest of your flock won't lamb for weeks. Do you have three more stalls left in the little barn?"

"We're full," James announced. "Ginny even moved Rose and the kittens into a wooden crate to free up a stall. When Sadie gets here, she can help us move the kittens into the farmhouse."

James stood, his hands on his hips, his eyes searching the neighboring woods. "It's not safe leaving the last three lambing ewes in the field. The bears are just coming out of hibernation and they're hungry. We better put the ewes in the big barn. I've never put animals in there before, but there's always a first time. I'll show you the other barn. We'll need to spread hay out and make some adjustments."

Bess walked alongside James as they strode across the field toward a big, red barn built a few hundred feet from the farmhouse. "Are you tired?" James asked. "You've had one strenuous day."

"I'm used to long hours, sometimes days without sleep," Bess admitted. "I've enjoyed today more than you can know. I feel more alive than I've felt for a very long time."

"Is it the sheep?" James asked.

"I enjoy being among the sheep, but you have a lot to do with it too," Bess assured him. "When I talk to you, everything seems to make more sense. I don't know how to explain it."

"We do have a connection," James admitted.

James opened the barn doors and walked into the warmth of the building. It was almost empty. A neat row of footlockers and trunks was all the building held. Bess walked toward the trunks noting they each had a name painted on the top.

"What is this place?" Bess asked, while looking around. "It's huge and almost empty. What's it for, James?"

"Mitchell and I designed this barn one long night in Afghanistan. It's where some of the guys and their families sleep and eat. They leave their things in a trunk or locker. Some like to pitch tents and camp out, but others stay in here, especially if it rains. It's big enough to provide shelter for the entire platoon and their families," James explained. "We store folding tables, chairs, and cots in the hay loft above us. We use a pulley system to lower them down on a platform."

"Is there hay in the hay loft?" Bess asked, with a grin on her face.

"Yes, there is hay up there," James said with a shrug. "I can see why you'd ask. This farm must seem odd to you."

"It's not like any farm I've ever been on, but I rather like it," Bess admitted. "You've got an assortment of animals, a tree house for your studio, and this barn for the men." She headed toward the steps to climb to the hayloft.

As he climbed the steps behind her, James agreed adding, "That's right. This barn was built for people. In April we'll hold Ginny's wedding and barbecue outside, weather permitting. If not, it will be in here. Either way, after the ceremony this place will be rocking with a good old-fashioned barn dance," James explained.

"Have you had one before?" Bess asked.

"We sure did," James said, as he pointed toward the bales of hay stacked in the corner. "In Afghanistan while they were planning activities, several of our men from Texas decided we should hold a square dance hoe-down at least once a year. We did just that in January. One of our guys is a trained caller and we had this place thumping. You should see how the kids picked it up," James added, as he threw the first bale of hay over the side."

"I love to square dance," Bess admitted as she shoved one over.

"Thought you might. Mitchell was really into it. He said we had to teach the easterners how it's done. We squared danced to Wayne's harmonica. You should have seen the soldiers promenading and circling around with each other. That's one of the good times that I like to remember when I think about our deployments. The guys would laugh, mock each other, and have a hell of a good time," James admitted.

"And in the meantime?" Bess asked as she shoved another bale of hay over the side. "What happens on this farm when the men and their families aren't here?"

"Nothing," James said as he looked around. "I guess nothing much. I paint and work with the animals. Ginny works on her computer. She's a consultant for several small companies and she waits for Mike."

"What are you waiting for?" Bess asked as she turned and sat down on a bale of hay.

"Me?" James asked, following her lead and sitting on one across from her. "I never thought about that. What about you? What are you waiting for?"

"I think the same thing you are," Bess said, picking a piece of hay out of the bale. She put it in her mouth and bit down on it, took it out and admitted, "I'm waiting for the memories to stop hurting so much. Everyone says time will dull the pain, but it hasn't yet. Sadie seems to be doing better than I am. She's talking now. She wants me to move on. I'm so relieved that she's doing better."

"How can I help?" James asked. "What can I do?"

"She wants to take pictures of Millie and Rascal. She's going to speak for the first time in school during Show and Tell when she shows the snapshots. She's going to tell them they can help her learn to talk better," Bess explained.

"They might ask why she stopped talking," James warned.

"I'm worried about the same thing," Bess said shaking her head. "I better warn her, but neither of us has ever talked to each other about that night."

"Maybe you should," James suggested. "When the guys come, we always have a barn fire off by ourselves. We talk about things that haunt us. We talk about how we're all dealing with the nightmares, the sweats, and the flashbacks. It helps us to talk it out," James confessed.

Bess took a long, deep breath. She closed her eyes and slowly shook her head. "Maybe it's time," she decided. "But I don't know how anyone finds the words?"

"I wonder if Sadie stopped talking for that very reason?" James guessed.

"You might be right?" Bess wondered as she slowly stood up. "Maybe I should help her find the words."

"Maybe," James said as he stood and moved next to Bess. He took her head gently in his hands and whispered, "Can I kiss you?"

"Yes," Bess said. "I'd like to be kissed."

Bess closed her eyes and tilted her head upwards. The aroma of the hay smelled familiar to her. The floorboards of the barn were similar to others she had stood upon. She steadied herself waiting for a familiar kiss. It wasn't. Nothing about it felt the same. His large hands cradled her face, a new sensation. His lips were thicker, softer, more exploratory than she'd experienced. They touched hers lightly, moving ever so slightly against hers. At first her lips tingled, then as the heat of their kiss rose, his hands dropped from her face and he pulled her toward him. Bess draped her arms around his neck, clutching him closer. As their lips pulsated against each other, her body shuddered in response. She felt intoxicated, dizzy, and disoriented.

They stepped back from each other, both breathing heavily, dazed by the exchange. Bess blinked and sat down on the bale of hay. She shook her head and whispered, "Wow."

James sat down across from her, adding another, "Wow."

They stared at each other, watching as they both struggled to gain control. Bess lifted her hands to her own cheeks and took in two deep breaths, then her eyes looked away while she processed what had happened.

When she looked back at him she smiled and said, "Sadie is coming soon. Fran is picking her up. I brought a camera so she could take pictures." She stood, started to slide the hay bale, then stopped reasoning, "I think you only need to have four more bales of hay thrown down." She brushed herself off, her hands noticeably shaking.

"I've got this. You go see if Sadie's here," James suggested. He stood and noticed Bess stepped back to put more room between them. It touched him.

Bess turned to leave. "Thanks, James," she mumbled as she quickly headed for the stairs. Her heart was still racing, and she knew she had to get out of there. She had to put distance between them. Her legs wobbled as she climbed down the stairs. Once on the main floor of the barn, she headed out the door running as fast as she could.

James watched from the loft above. He smiled, thinking, "She's always running to or from something. Wonder if I can get her to stop?"

Half an hour later, Fran's car pulled into the driveway. Bess was in the goat pasture, checking Dispy over. Sadie and Judy came running toward her. "Mom, did you see the kittens yet?" Sadie asked.

"No, Sadie. I've been working with the sheep and goats. I wanted to wait for you. Hi, Judy. Did you get a kitten the other day?" Bess asked.

"No, I want one from the same litter as Sadie's. I'm gonna pick it out today," Judy announced, a grin on her face.

"It's all she talks about," Fran added as she and Ginny caught up. "How's it going? Are all the sheep done lambing?"

"For now," Bess said. "I was just checking over the goats."

"Can you tell James how to make their milk taste better?" Ginny asked. "We can't even give our goat milk away."

"I better focus on the sheep for now. A few more ewes will lamb later tonight," Bess explained.

"Maybe you should stay here in case they do," Fran suggested. "I'll take Sadie home with us and she can have a pajama party with Judy."

"Pwease Mom, can we do that?" Sadie begged. "Pwease!"

James walked up just in time to hear them begging. "Hi Fran. I'm glad you brought Judy and Sadie over. The kittens need to be moved into the farmhouse and we've been too busy. What's going on here?"

Sadie ran up to James extending her arms for him to pick her up. He didn't, instead he stooped down so he could talk to both girls at one time. Bess appreciated his action. Her one-track mind had switched gears, and she was now focused only on Sadie. The same protective instinct had emerged, and she was watching her daughter's every move for signs of any growing dependency toward James.

"Miss Fwan wants me to spend the night with Judy," Sadie informed James as both girls moved closer to him. "I didn't bwing my pj's" Sadie realized, as she turned toward Judy.

"You can borrow some of mine. I've got three pairs," Judy announced.

James' eyes lifted to look at Bess, a grin on his face, "What does your Mom have to say about that?" he asked.

Bess had been watching just Sadie, until she heard his question. She moved her focus to James and a thrill of expectation raced through her body. "I was just about to say that's a good idea. I can stay in case the sheep need me. The rest of the sheep won't have their lambs for another few weeks," she announced.

"Can I have one of the kittens?" Judy asked James.

"That's up to Sadie," James answered. "She's the one who really saved them. If Sadie hadn't known Cricket was having babies, her mom wouldn't have known to look for them."

"Weawwy? Them's all mine?" Sadie said, stunned.

"You and your mom's. You both promised Cricket you'd find good homes for them, remember?" James said.

"Yup, we did," Sadie said happily. "I think you shouwd take the wast two. Then they can pway togethea when you is gone to schoow," Sadie reasoned.

"That might be a good idea," Fran admitted. "Your brother said he'd like a kitten too. All he does now is smack everything, lacrosse season you know," Fran added. "A kitten might put him back in touch with his softer side."

"Wet's go wook at them," Sadie yelled, as she led the way for Judy to follow.

Bess watched and shook her head sadly. "Wait till Sadie sees all the lambs in the barn. She hasn't gone near lambs in two years. I don't know what to expect."

"Didn't she help with the lambs at your farm?" Fran asked.

"Sadie loved the lambs, fed the orphaned lambs bottles, played with them all the time. She hasn't gone near them since the death of her father," Bess said looking toward the sheep in the field, "Sadie blames sheep for his death. Seeing the lambs might put her into a flashback."

"Should we go with them?" James asked, growing concerned.

"Yes, but not right away," Bess said in almost a whisper. "I think she needs to figure this out on her own. Judy's with her. This might be the perfect way for Sadie to finally deal with her anger. Let's just walk slowly toward the barn, let them see we don't think there's a reason to hurry along," Bess suggested.

Eleven

"Them's in the wittwe barn," Sadie announced to Judy. "The wast two are wewwy cute. One is a bwown tabby and one is gway with bwack spots."

"I can't wait," Judy said, so they started to run.

Sadie swung the door open carefully, and they walked inside. As her eyes scanned the stalls filled with ewes and nursing lambs, she yelled, "What happened? Sheep and wambs awe hewe!"

"I love sheep and lambs," Judy exclaimed. "Look how cute they are! James lets us play with them. Come look," Judy urged, pushing past Sadie and running up to the first stall. "This one is so tiny."

"I hate wambs," Sadie asserted, as tears rose to her eyes. She began backing up, ending in a crouching position on a pile of straw in the corner.

"Don't be afraid," Judy called back. "Look, the little one is sucking my finger."

The baas of the twenty-two sheep seemed deafening to Sadie. She covered her ears and began rocking back and forth, humming to drown out their sound. Judy ran up to her, crouched and asked, "What's wrong? They're so cute. Come look!"

"No, I hate them!" Sadie said. "They kiwwed my dad!"

Judy grew afraid, cuddling up next to Sadie. "I didn't know sheep can kill people," she squealed. "Did they kick him?"

"No," Sadie said, just as Bess, Fran, Ginny, and James walked in and spotted the two crouched kids. They froze, carefully assessing the situation.

"Do they bite?" Judy asked, unaware of the adults.

"No," Sadie admitted. "Sheep don't bite. They butt you with their heads if they want to tell you something."

"They butted your dad real hard?" Judy asked, still cuddled up with closed eyes next to Sadie.

"No. That's siwwy," Sadie admitted.

"Then how did they kill your dad?" Judy asked, opening her eyes.

Sadie grew quiet, then opened her eyes. She looked at her friend, tilting her head. Her shoulders dropped, and Bess knew her daughter needed help to find the words.

"Sadie's dad was a shepherd," Bess said, as she moved toward the two girls. "He loved our sheep. We had lots of them, over three hundred." She sat cross-legged, facing the girls. "We lived on a 3,000 acre farm that had been in our family since the 1900s. We left many acres of our land for the wildlife so the land would stay the way it was before our family came there."

"That's right," Sadie agreed, her eyes urging Bess to continue.

"We had chickens, roosters, goats, horses, and a guard llama named Juan," Bess explained. "Sadie milked her goat and got all our eggs."

"My goat miwk tasted much better than Dipsy's," Sadie bragged. The adults laughed and sat down on bales of hay close to the children.

"Did you have a dog like Shep?" Judy asked.

"No," Bess admitted "We did at one time, but our flock thought I was their sheepdog."

"All Mama had to do was wawk into the fiewd and aww the sheep came running. They woved Mama. She was a shephewd too. Daddy had another job," Sadie explained. "He made money taking cawe of the woads."

"It's hard to make money raising sheep," Bess said looking over at James. "You have to work hard to make ends meet. You have to look at it like a business, not a hobby. Mitchell taught us that."

Bess turned back and smiled at the girls. "We liked living on the farm, didn't we?" Bess asked Sadie.

"We did," Sadie admitted.

"How could you if you hate sheep?" Judy asked. "You had so many."

"I didn't hate sheep then," Sadie admitted. "I wasn't mad at them then. I took good cawe of the ones whose mothews died or wouldn't feed them. Didn't I?" Sadie asked her mother, pride on her face.

"Very good care," Bess said smiling. "Sometimes Sadie had ten little lambs that counted on her to feed them. We made a little, fenced-in pasture by the house so Sadie could go there and take care of her sheep. She had a little house so she could bring in one sheep at a time and she would sit on a bench and feed them a bottle. If she hadn't had the little house, what would they do to you?"

"They would aww twy to get me to feed them. They wuvved me so much," Sadie said beaming.

"You were so lucky," Judy said.

"I was veawy wucky," Sadie admitted. "I had two kittens too. My pony was weal wittwe and I called hew Pwincess," Sadie explained. "She was spotted. My fweind, Singing Biwd, gave her to me. We wouwd wide togethea aww the time on my fawm or hew wesewvation."

"I wouldn't leave that fawm," Judy said enthralled.

Sadie's head dropped, so Bess asked, "Before I tell why we left, I think you two should go get the kittens. I need to hold my Callie while I tell that part of the story. Do you want to hold Millie?"

Sadie looked up and whispered, "Can you do it, Momma? Can you teww the stowy?"

"I think it will be good to tell the story," Bess said holding her head high. "Don't you?"

Sadie looked over at Judy and warned her. "It's vewy scawwy. Do you want to heaw it?"

"I watch scary movies with my brother. Boys like scary stuff. Let's go get our kittens first," Judy said jumping to her feet.

"I'll take you to them," Ginny suggested as she led them toward the other end of the little barn.

Bess stood and stretched, watching her daughter stop at a stall. Then Sadie slowly opened the door and walked toward the sheep. Judy watched her and followed her lead. "You always ask the mamma fiwst if you can pet them, wike this," Sadie instructed. "Can I pet youw babies?" Sadie asked reaching out to pat the ewe on the head. The ewe baaed affectionally and the two children dropped to their knees to caress the soft baby lambs.

"You like them now?" Judy asked before nuzzling her face close to the little baaing lamb facing her.

"Sheep are good. They're weawwy vewy woving and kind," Sadie admitted. The wams are mean. Don't evewa pet a wam."

"What's a wam?" Judy asked.

"A rrram," Sadie said very carefully. "It's a boy sheep. They're grouchy."

"Like my brother," Judy said, and they both fell into a fit of laughter.

"You've been doing great!" James said softly. "Are you good to go on?"

"It seems so natural here, in this barn surrounded by the lambs and their mothers. Having all of you here helps too. I know you have my back if I mess up," Bess admitted.

"You couldn't mess up," James assured her. "All you need to do is tell your truth. She's made up her own. Her memories might be very different. Soldiers find that out all the time. It's just the way it is. So many guys are shocked when they hear someone else's version. They've blocked out facts, sometimes made them worse."

"Thanks, James," Bess whispered as she watched Sadie and Judy run towards the kittens. "Could there be a better place for us than this?"

James heard her words, and turned to stare at her. Bess was oblivious to what she had said. He smiled thinking, *If only you really felt that way. If only.*

Bess wondered if Sadie would return to the corner to hear about her father's death. She had decided she wouldn't push her if she chose not to. It didn't take long, however, before Sadie ran back to her mom, Callie in one arm, Millie in the other. She lifted Callie toward her mom saying, "Cawwie will help you. You can cuddle hew in the hawd pawts."

"Thank you, honey. Millie will help you," Bess promised. Sadie sat down, Judy running to join her. She'd picked the grey, spotted kitten and her face beamed with happiness. Bess turned and saw James stroking Junior and Fran cuddling the remaining kitten.

Bess sat back down cross-legged, kissing Callie gently and holding her like a baby. Callie purred and Bess began saying, "It was

March, and it had been cold the entire month. Living with so much wildlife around us was challenging. We often saw mountain lions, coyotes, eagles, and grizzly bears, especially during cold springs like the one we were having. There was so little food, and they all had babies of their own to feed."

Bess looked away and lifted Callie to her lips, kissing her softly, feeling her little body vibrate as she purred. She continued saying, "We put our sheep into a long building every night to keep them safe."

"All momma had to do was stand thewe and the sheep aww came wunning, then she'd walk to the building and they'd fow-wow hew. They'd wun inside and stay aww nice and wawm," Sadie explained proudly. She dropped her eyes and added, "Then the snow came."

"The animals that lived around us could get in the barn if they really wanted to," Bess continued. "These were wild, western animals; some had lived in the mountain caves sleeping throughout the winter months. We used electric fences to keep the grizzly bears out."

Only the animals moved and made noises. The humans all waited for Bess to continue. "Sadie's dad had to clear the snow off the highway. It was his job, but the snow kept falling. It was a spring blizzard, it dumped several feet of snow, but it also brought a thunderstorm."

"While it was snowing?" Judy asked.

"Yes, while it snowed. We felt the lightning hit, then all our electricity went out. Sadie and I were home alone, and we used candles and a lantern to see," Bess explained.

"We had a big fiwe in the fiwepwace," Sadie added. We stayed wawm by the fiwa."

"Sadie's dad had worked twelve hours straight, but he got to come home to check up on us and the sheep," Bess said.

"Dad came home and I sat on his wap while he ate mommas's wamb stew. Momma, why don't you make wamb stew anymowe?" Sadie asked, looking up at Bess.

"We'll have to buy some lamb from James," Bess said gently.

Ginny said, "Good luck with that. James doesn't sell lamb."

"With a flock this big, you better start," Bess suggested, and then noticed James flinch.

"Teww the west, Momma," Sadie urged, to the shock of everyone.

Bess shook her head *yes*, took a deep breath and continued, "Drew, Sadie's dad, was still in all his warm clothes from plowing snow. He knew the lambs and sheep would be in trouble if the bears sensed the electric fences were off, so he took his rifle and told us he'd spend the night in the barn."

"I towd him not to go," Sadie said, her big, blue eyes tearing up. "I towd him to wet the big beaws have the sheep."

"I forgot that," Bess said amazed. "You did, didn't you?"

"Daddy said he had to go 'cause a shephewd has to take cawe of his fwock," Sadie said. "I towd him he shouwd take cawe of me fiwst."

"What did your daddy say then?" Judy asked.

"He said Momma can take cawe of me. Then wemember what daddy said?" Sadie asked Bess.

"He said to not leave the house no matter what we hear," Bess said slowly, reliving the moment.

"Momma didn't wisten to my daddy," Sadie said. "Hews took me and we got in the twuck and went to that bawn. We went when we heawd the beaw growling," Sadie added.

"I should have listened to your daddy," Bess said, dropping her head.

"No, Momma," Sadie said lifting Millie and rubbing the kitten across her own cheek. "You were a hewo. You kiwwed the beaw that was eating daddy."

While others gasped, Bess stared in disbelief at Sadie. "No, Sadie. I'm not a hero. You're the hero," she yelled.

"You shot the beaw," Sadie said, standing up and moving next to her mom.

"No, Sadie. I got out of the truck and then I couldn't move. I just stood there. The grizzly bear turned to look at me and growled. He was going to kill me," Bess said, up on her knees, her hands on her daughter's shoulders. "You were four years old but you saved me," Bess said. "Remember what you did?"

"No, Mamma, I was too wittwe," Sadie said slowly.

"You beeped the truck horn. Over and over again, you beeped the truck horn. It made me brave so then I shot the bear," Bess said. "You were the hero."

"But I didn't save my daddy," Sadie said crying.

"Your daddy was gone before we got there," Bess said, hugging her.

"The bear ate my daddy," Sadie said crying.

Bess moved Sadie an arm's length away. She looked into her eyes and said very slowly. "Your daddy wasn't eaten by the bear. He was probably in the truck with you, telling you to beep the horn. He was taking care of you, like you asked him too," Bess said carefully.

"He was taking cawe of me," Sadie said, "and you."

"Yes," Bess said, "and he wanted us to be safe and happy."

"It's not the sheep's fault daddy's dead. Is it Momma?" Sadie asked.

"No. It's no one's fault, but you kept me alive," Bess said, hugging her little girl. "You are a true hero."

Judy ran up to Sadie, hugging her. "You're the bravest girl I ever knew."

"If you two help me move the kittens and Rose into the house, I'll make everyone hot chocolate," Ginny said, through red, tearstained eyes.

"I'm so sorry, Bess," James said once everyone else left the barn. "I can't imagine going through that."

"I was only picturing the bear clawing and biting Drew, but now I realize it is like I said. He wasn't there. I should have realized that Drew was really with Sadie in that truck. She'd never beeped that horn in her life. It had to be him; it's the only way she'd have known to do that," Bess said, relief in her face.

"I believe you're right," James said. "It had to be him."

"I feel like a heavy weight has been lifted off my heart," Bess said. "Drew was my best friend. I couldn't stand the thought of him suffering."

"I don't think he felt a thing," James encouraged.

"No, probably didn't even see the bear. He hadn't even taken his gun off his shoulder. It just laid there next to him," Bess said remembering.

"A matter of seconds," James said sadly. "That's what we tell each other. Death can take just a matter of seconds–so quick the brain doesn't even get the message. You die oblivious, no fear, no pain."

"Thank God," Bess whispered.

"Maybe you should go home with Sadie. You two might need to be together," James suggested.

"No, separating from Sadie is a good idea. We both need time to process what we talked about. It's better for us to be with people who weren't there and *don't have a nickel in the dime*," Bess decided.

"I like that saying," James said. "Might use that myself sometime."

"It was one of my Dad's favorites," Bess said shrugging. "Feel free. He'd have liked that." She looked up at James adding, "He'd have liked you."

"He'd probably have thought I was a dumb Greenhorn," James suggested shaking his head.

"Yes, you are that," Bess admitted, "but you have courage and you are a man of your word. I wonder if Mitchell thought you would do this without him?"

"He knew I would," James said smiling. "The deal was: if I died, The Funny Farm was going to be in Montana."

"So he knew it would be here in Pennsylvania if he died," Bess continued. "Where was it going to be if you both lived?"

"Here in Pennsylvania," James admitted. "He'd visited me once when he was on leave. Wanted to see where the *city boy* lived. That's what he called me."

"Were you a *city boy?*" Bess asked.

"Sure was. Grew up on the streets of York. My idea of gathering vegetables for dinner was going to Central Market and buying them from the vendors," James admitted.

"And now?" Bess asked as she stood up and moved toward the door.

"Now I live off the land. Get my vegetables from my own garden. During growing season, I take a load in twice a week to the Food Bank. I want the *city kids* to learn how good fresh vegetables can be," James admitted, as they began walking toward the pasture. "That's what I spent all my time reading up on. I was going to be the farm expert. Mitchell was going to take care of the sheep and goats. I've got a lot to learn about the animals."

"Think what you've done in a year or so. You bought the land, supervised the building of everything on this farm, planted vegetables, and in just one month you'll have the largest flock of Blue Faced Leicester on the East Coast," Bess advised him.

"What?" James asked shocked. "You're kidding, right? I don't want the biggest flock of sheep."

"Then we better talk about that later on. You could end up with six hundred sheep by May," Bess said before she tilted her head and teased. "How about that, *city boy?*" James watched in stunned silence as Bess ran off toward the sheep. *Six hundred sheep? I don't want six hundred sheep!* he thought, his heartbeat racing. *What the hell am I going to do with all those sheep?*

James stood shaking his head in disgust until he noticed the movements in the field. Bess had stopped running a few hundred feet ahead of James. She lifted her fingers to her mouth and gave out a long whistle. Shep, Rascal, and Big Bertha reacted, stopping frozen in their tracks. The sheep all took notice, flocking together, obeying their natural instinct for protection, except the ewes with yarn around their necks. They separated from the flock and moved toward the red-haired woman who had been palpating and talking to them gently. They knew Bess was there to help them lamb.

In less than ten minutes, the lambing ewes, with help from Shep, were staying in line behind Bess as she walked toward the barn. *That is one special woman*, James thought, as he hurried to open the barn doors.

"How'd you do that?" James asked, as they followed her into the barn. "They don't know you!"

"Sheep get a bad rap for being stupid because they stay flocked together and seldom act independently," Bess explained. "They only stay together for self-preservation. Truth is, sheep are very smart. It's been proven that sheep can reason and react as well as monkeys, rodents, and in some tests, humans." Bess helped the sheep relax on the soft hay before adding, "They have advanced learning capabilities and can problem solve."

"That smart, but why do they follow you?" James protested.

"They know they're getting ready to lamb and they're nervous. They watched me help other ewes lambing, and I've handled each of these sheep a few times. They can tell I want to help them. They've imprinted my face," Bess said as she looked into the eyes of a thankful ewe. She patted its head and it baaed happily.

Bess continued saying, "I once sold some sheep to a rancher in east Montana. Sadie and I stopped to drop off the last of our flock and our former sheep came running. They spotted us from across the field, and it had been almost two years since they'd seen us."

"You're kidding, right?" James asked.

"I'm serious. I wouldn't give you bad information. Sheep can remember human faces for years, if they've made some attachment to you. One researcher proved that years after they've been separated, sheep remember the faces of over fifty sheep who'd been in their flock."

"And you want me to butcher them?" James asked with a grin.

"A topic for another day," Bess said, stroking one ewe. "This ewe is about to become the mother of triplets. Aren't you lucky?" she laughed as she sat down on the straw and caught one lamb as it slid easily into the world.

They sat in the barn, waiting for the next two to be born. "It could be a while," Bess warned. "I brought a pair of my monitors. They're in my trunk. We could put one with them, keep one, and then go milk the goats," Bess suggested.

"I can go get the monitors," James said standing.

Bess handed him her keys, asking, "I keep a change of clothing in a blue bag in the trunk. I think I'll need it. I feel grungy," Bess admitted.

"You look anything but grungy," James said, as he stood and looked down at her.

"How tall are you?" Bess asked as she stared up at him.

"Six feet, two inches," James admitted. "I figured you to be a good foot shorter than me."

"So you've been sizing me up, have you?" Bess asked smiling.

"Yes, I have," James admitted. "You're beautiful inside and out, thin but strong. I'll throw a few potatoes in the oven just in case we have time to eat after I milk. I'll grill up two steaks for dinner."

"Let me guess," Bess said laughing, "with vegetables from your garden."

"Absolutely," James said proudly, as he walked away. "I hope you like salads; it's too early for much else."

"I love vegetables," Bess said with a laugh. "Don't let Sadie leave without saying goodbye to me, please."

"I'll send her your way," James promised.

"Is she having mowe wambs, Mama?" Sadie asked, as she sat down by Bess.

"Two more," Bess explained as she hugged her daughter. "Do you still want to spend the night with Judy?"

"Yes, Mama," Sadie said smiling. "She's gonna paint my naiws pink."

"Wonderful," Bess simply said.

"Will you be hewe tomorrow?" Sadie asked.

"Yes," I'll be here," Bess said gently. "You haven't had a chance to see Rascal today. Tomorrow we'll take those pictures you want and then we'll take them to the drug store and get your copies made for school."

"Can I go to the wacrosse game with Miss Fwan and Miss Ginny? Judy's bwother is pwaying. Will I wike a wacrosse game, Mama?" Sadie asked.

"It'll be fun to watch all the people walking around, and maybe they'll have a band play a song and march onto the field," Bess said trying to imagine what a lacrosse game would be like. "Why is Ginny going?"

"It's at the school Miss Ginny used to go to. She was a cheew-weader when she was in that school," Sadie explained. "Then she's going to spend the night with Miss Fwan. She's gonna show us how to cheew. Miss Fwan and Ginny awe gonna watch giwl movies. They awe vewy excited."

"Well, you should all have a good time," Bess said hugging Sadie.

"Awe you sad you can't come?" Sadie asked.

"You know how much I like to be with sheep." Bess said smiling.

"Okay, then I'll go," Sadie said. "I know you wuvv being with sheep the best, except fow me," Sadie admitted before kissing her mom and running out of the barn.

"James," Bess called into the monitor. "Did you hear all that?"

"Sure did," James admitted. "These monitors work perfectly. "I've started milking. The potatoes are cooking; all is well," he answered.

"Do you think everyone is leaving so we can be alone?" Bess asked.

"I was wondering the same thing," James admitted. "Don't feel pressured about anything, Bess. We can just relax and enjoy the night."

"Wait, here come the lambs," Bess said quietly. "Good girl, Mama. That's a girl. Now one big push, Mama. There you go. James, it's a ram! This one goes to the butcher. It has a bad leg. Here comes the last one. Come, Mama, last one and then you rest," Bess instructed. "It's a beautiful ewe."

"Great news. Is that how you decide who goes to the butcher?" James asked.

"Yes, you have a responsibility to only sell perfect examples of the breed. I think you should sell lambs to Montana so they can start breeding Blue Faced Leisters. Mitchell would have liked that," Bess suggested.

"You're absolutely right. What a great idea," James said, as he kept his pace milking. "Any more good ideas?"

"Yes, since you asked. Mitchell used to say that you only keep the animals that you want on the farm. He warned us not to keep too many; they become a burden. You don't need all these sheep," Bess said.

"No, I don't," James admitted. "What do you suggest?"

"I suggest you keep no more than fifty Blue Faced Leisters. Sell, butcher, or give the rest away. That will be easy to do. Then I think you need about thirty Shetland sheep. They're little mountain sheep, very self-reliant. Most of all, they don't have as many lambs. Besides that, you're a painter. You should have sheep of different colors with different faces. That's the Shetland. You'd enjoy painting Shetland sheep," Bess suggested. "They're still fiber sheep, so you can keep them for years."

"I feel my blood pressure going down already," James admitted. "Thanks, Bess. I can't tell you how much you're coming here has meant to me. I wish there was something I could do for you."

"There is," Bess admitted. "I'd like to take a bath before dinner. Is that possible?"

"Sure is," James said after a pause. "I'm used to doing all the milking on my own. I have a big soaking tub in my bedroom. Feel free to use it."

"What's a soaking tub?" Bess asked, as she worked to settle the lambs next to their mother.

"It's a tub big enough for two people. The builder said I had to put it in since I was a bachelor," James admitted.

"Why?" Bess asked. "How's it different than a regular tub?"

"It's supposed to fit two people," James said after a pause.

Quiet filled the air waves. "Oh," she finally said. "Don't you have a regular tub? I don't want to waste water."

"That's how I feel every time I need a bath. I use the shower. Please use that damn thing. I don't even know if it works," James admitted.

"Well, if you don't mind," Bess said. "Do you get your water from a well?"

"Yes, and I have more water than I'll ever need. Soak away. I'll listen for the other lambs. It's the least I can do for you," James added.

"You're cooking for me too," Bess said after another pause.

"Yes, I will cook for you," James added. "Anything else?"

"Yes, we'll be alone, James. I think you should show me around your house, and then I'd like to see your tree house," Bess said through the monitor.

"Are you sure?" James asked carefully.

"No, but I'm trying very hard to be seductive. I hope you want to be with me," Bess asked.

"I've wanted you from the first time I saw you running toward Cricket," James admitted. "It's all I can do not to run to the barn and take you in my arms," he added.

"James," her voice said through the monitor. "I'm leaving now. I'll be in your bath tub, if you need me."

Thirteen

Bess approached the steps to the farmhouse and studied the structure thinking, *It could be a beautiful house. It has all the components, a big front porch and decorative molding; but the house looks pale, bland, and lifeless.* She studied it, shaking her head. *It lacks color, just as Ginny said. No wonder I didn't give it a second glance.*

Bess walked up the stairs, crossed the empty porch thinking, *it needs a porch swing, maybe a few chairs and a small table.* She took off her boots, leaving them next to Ginny's. Bess opened the front door expecting the same bland interior, but she was both surprised and relieved to find the opposite.

She stood mesmerized, as the door swung closed behind her. Inside, the color palette reflected James' love of nature. The floors were covered in warm, earth-toned oak with oriental rugs placed in seating areas. The few walls were each painted varying shades of complementary colors, moldings painted carmel broke the visual tension usually created when bold colors connected. The ceiling was painted a light, periwinkle blue to mimic the sky.

The harmonious color scheme soothed Bess' senses. *These are all the colors in my wardrobe,* Bess realized. *Every color I'm drawn to: rust, green, gold, pumpkin, with accents of turquoise.* She took in a deep, relaxing breath, smelling the burning wood in the fireplace, the baking potatoes, and the fresh herbs gathered for the salad. The soft meows from the basket of kittens tucked behind a makeshift barrier completed the calming effect on all her senses.

The open-concept floor plan allowed the inhabitants to move freely between designated areas of the kitchen, living, and dining room. Soft, molasses-colored leather furniture with hand woven, Native American-patterned pillows sat around the stone fireplace with its crackling logs. Her fingers trailed across the butter-soft sofa.

Realistic paintings adorned the walls, a cream sheep standing in the morning mist, a floppy-eared goat perched on top of a wood pile, Big, Bad Bertha chasing a coyote, and a ewe nursing two lambs. Each canvas was simply signed "James". The honest portraits captured the essence of each critter and brought tears to her eyes.

She opened one of the two doors to find Ginny's bedroom and connecting bath. She shut it quickly. Bess decided that the main sleeping area must be on the second floor, and she climbed the stairs in search of his bedroom.

The first three rooms were essentially empty, only a bed and dresser set up in one. Bess resigned herself that she'd made a mistake coming upstairs until she opened the last door and knew it was his room. It looked like him: bold, masculine, organized, and comfortable, with a king-size bed against the apple-green wall and another oriental rug on the brown, oak floor. The bed was made up with perfectly squared corners, military style. One closet door was open and Bess walked over, amazed at the precision with which all the garments were hung. *Military training*, she thought.

Bess wandered into the large master bathroom. A tile shower with a glass door stood in one corner, two beige sinks were set in the granite counter, a mirror covering the wall above. A commode stood across from the sinks and in the far corner a huge 60" by 60" whirlpool, corner tub seemed to be waiting for her arrival.

Bess moved toward it, bent over and turned on the water. The air in the pipes proved James had never used the tub as did the unused bottle of bubble bath. She opened it, poured some in and took off her clothes, folding them and putting them to the side.

I've got nothing to put on, she realized. While water filled the tub, Bess returned to his bedroom and selected a flannel shirt from the closet. Her eyes caught her image in the mirror. She stepped forward staring at the reflection of her nude body, clutching his shirt with his bed behind her. Her heartbeat skipped and her rose-colored nipples grew erect in front of her own eyes. Bess turned, crossed to his bed, picked up his pillow and drew in the scent. Goose bumps covered her arms; her breath caught in her throat. Startled, she replaced it and moved quickly back to the bathroom.

Bess slid into the hot bathwater, grateful when her body relaxed. The tub had been designed with two seats, one beside the other. She smiled, wondering how it would feel to have James seated next to her, cloaked only in warm water. Bess picked up a handful of bubbles and lifted them to her nose. *Eucalyptus,* she thought. She looked for a bar of soap and spotted three buttons. She pushed one and warm water shot out from various vents, messaging her muscles and creating whirls. The bubbles tripled in number and Bess laughed, relaxed, and let the flow wash over her.

After a while, curiosity got the better of Bess and she pushed the next button. Six blue lights appeared below the surface of the water. She looked through the thick layer of bubbles, amazed how the tub now resembled the aqua waters in magazine pictures of the tropics.

Her focus shifted when she heard his footsteps on the stairs. Bess lowered her head below the water, letting her hair become washed in the eucalyptus aroma he must like. She re-emerged, removed the water and bubbles from her face with her hands and then settled back in her seat, waiting and hoping he would come to her.

"Bess, I brought you up a glass of wine," James said tentatively from just outside the bathroom door. "Shall I bring it in?"

"I hope you brought two, one for you," Bess admitted. "I've been waiting for you."

A few minutes elapsed and Bess waited in tense expectation. When the door did open, James came in holding two glasses of wine, dressed in only his partly unbuttoned shirt. His eyes grew wide as he saw her, bottom lit in soft blue, surrounded by whirling bubbles whose pungent scent drew him nearer. Her long, red hair was wet, radiant in comparison to the white and blue. Her big, brown eyes were open wide, roaming over his partially exposed body. Her lips were partially open to assist her heavy breathing.

There was no hiding his own arousal, so no words were necessary. He placed the glasses on the wide tub surround and removed his shirt, looking at what he could see of Bess' naked body beneath the water. Then James sat on the edge of the tub, leaned over and gently kissed her awaiting lips. Her arms reached up to encircle his neck, her full, naked breasts rising above the water and rubbing against his chest. James eased back, both his hands reaching out to take one and then he caressed them, groaning as he did.

Bess arched back, her head resting against the back of her seat, letting her brain register all the sensations aroused in the sensitive nerve endings within her bosom. The feel of the pulsating water, his warm, gentle hands stroking and teasing her nipples almost brought her to climax. She opened her eyes and whispered, "James."

Within seconds, he was next to her, his long, lean body rolling over hers in a water ballet unlike either had ever experienced. Her hands rushed to his chest, tracing the tiger line of chest hair that ran from the top of his torso to his waist, then down to his groin. Her fingertips returned to examine and knead his nipples and pectoral muscles.

James slipped into the seat beside her, lifting her gently with him, until she sat on top. He stared into her eyes as she groaned and looked down at him, saying, "Your body's as perfect as your face. James, you're driving me insane."

Bess could wait no longer; she lifted herself up and then lowered down onto him, reveling in the depth with which he entered. His hands grabbed her butt, his fingers pulsated her skin, his arms began raising and lowering her while she leaned forward, enabling him to suck on one of her nipples as she grabbed onto his thick, wet hair. The noise of the bubbles, moving water, and tub filter could not drown out both their cries as they undulated to the thumping rhythm of their sexual needs. Their final chorus was achieved in perfect harmony.

They lay back in the seats, both gasping for air, as their heartbeats slowed to normal. Finally, Bess reached up and pushed the first button; the jet streams slowed and the swirls became ripples. She pressed the second button and the color turned from blue to green. They both laughed.

"What a way to break in this crazy thing," James said. "What happens if you press that button again?"

Bess did and the water turned yellow. She pressed it again and it became purple. "I like blue; what about you?" she asked.

"Blue, definitely blue," he agreed as he looked up at the ceiling and relaxed until he sat up and asked, "Bess, could you get pregnant under water?"

"I don't know," Bess admitted, a look of panic covering her face. Then he saw her smile and relax. "We're safe," she said taking in a deep breath. "My cycle stopped and my doctor didn't know if it was because of stress or the depression medicine. He put me on birth control pills to regulate it." She looked over at James admitting, "I hated taking those things. It was like swallowing a reminder that Sadie would never have any siblings and I would never have sex. Now I'm very grateful I didn't stop." They both laughed.

"Good thing," James said. "Not that I wouldn't like to have kids running around."

"Is that why you built this house with four bedrooms upstairs and the guest room on the first floor?" Bess asked.

"Yup," James admitted. "I don't plan to ever move from this farm. Thought I better build this house so it could fit my dream family. This farm means more to me than just fulfilling a promise. It grounds me, makes me feel more in control in a world gone wild. Here I can live honestly, not relying on a society designed around a weird economic structure set up to make its architects wealthy. I can do work that makes me proud and still pay the mortgage. I feel safe living this life."

"I used to agree with you," Bess said. "Never imagined living anywhere but our farm." He watched as she took her hands and pushed the water away until it splashed. She took in a deep breath. "A farm isn't safe. You can't control your own fate. Mother nature does. A long drought, disease, blizzard, flood, hurricane, or hungry bears can take it all away."

"I can't imagine how hard it was to move from your farm. You said it had been in your family for generations," James said, reaching out to hold her hand.

"I couldn't stay there, neither could Sadie. I'll never let myself get that rooted to anything again," she announced as she eased her hand from his grasp, using it to brush the bubbles back from her body. "I was willing to pour my sweat and tears into that farm, but when I saw Drew's blood seeping into the dirt, I hated it. Couldn't get far enough away."

They sat with only the hum of the gurgling bathtub breaking the silence. Finally James asked, "Does that mean you would never start over with someone like me?"

"I couldn't, James," Bess said, looking into his eyes. "I only have energy for Sadie. Nothing else is left. I warned you about that. I'm being honest."

"One thing at a time?" James asked. "Have you always been this way?"

"No," Bess admitted, "only after Drew died. There were days that I couldn't move out of bed. Just laid there. My cousin came over to take care of Sadie and me. Then Singing Bird and her father came to visit. Did you know I'm one-quarter Native American?" she asked as she carefully passed a glass of wine over to him. She repositioned herself in the tub to sit cross-legged facing him with her glass of wine safely in her hand.

"I can see that now that you mention it. You have high cheekbones," James said smiling, toasting, and then sipping his wine.

"Her father is the chief and a very wise man," Bess said before taking a sip. "His council saved me. He looked down at me and said, *Be like the fox. Take one step at a time; do one thing at a time. Don't lose focus from that one thing. Then you will survive.*"

"So that's how you live now?" James said watching her.

"Yes, and Sadie is my one thing. Everything I do is for her," Bess said, until she hesitated and took another long sip. "Well, what just happened between us had nothing to do with Sadie," she added blushing as she looked into his eyes.

"I'm sure all the wise foxes take every opportunity to do this as often as possible," he assured her. "What were you like before taking his advice?"

"You mean before the bear?" Bess asked. James nodded and Bess thought. "I was an entrepreneur. I made goat milk soap with fresh herbs from my garden. My cousin owns a small store in town where she sells baked goods. I became her partner and sold my things. I kept her shelves stocked with my homemade soaps, sheepskins, and various types of yarn."

She smiled and drank more wine, thinking back to better times, "I sold my hand-spun yarn and then I designed mule-spun yarn from my fleece. It was made in a Canadian mill. I developed a beautiful line in the colors of Montana. My favorite thing about fiber is the dying of it. I developed the perfect formula to duplicate all the colors found in nature around me. The yarn became so popular that I had a large, mail-order business. Made enough to pay for all my animals and then some."

James watched as the life came back into her eyes. She sat forward, her free hand waving above the aqua water as she explained all the colors of her homeland. In those few minutes, he glimpsed the woman she had been: in charge, confident, excited by life, and the world around her.

She stopped talking, pausing as a thought invaded her conversation. She looked at him and the conversation took a turn. "You could turn your fleece into your own brand of yarn. You could name all the colors from the wonders on the east coast," she suggested. Now her hand moved as if she was picking colors out of the atmosphere. She began a list saying, "New York steel, it would be a silver gray, heavy on the black pigments; Cape Cod blue, heavy on the indigo; Smoky Mountain green; you'd have to add white to the green; Florida tropics," she said, splashing the aqua water toward him."

James reached out and took her wine glass. He carefully placed both glasses on the shelf. His hands reached out for Bess and gently eased her forward until she laid on top of him. "You're just a little thing, aren't you? Look, your feet come to my knees," he said as his hands rubbed down her back and over her butt.

"We seem to match up where necessary," Bess said, as she felt his arousal return.

"You're one amazing woman," James admitted. She began floating back and forth above him, and he closed his eyes thinking, *you belong right here. We belong together—you, me, and Sadie.*

Fourteen

Bess lay perfectly still, the deep slumber paralyzing her voluntary muscles while her respiration rate, eye movement, and brain activity increased. Bess was dreaming.

They were all around her, their grazing stopped, their cream faces oozing love, trust, and devotion. All were bleating, the chorus of baaas sounding like a hymn. It was peaceful here in this field of sheep. She knew them all by name like family members never to be forgotten. This was a good place, blissful and safe. She saw movement; it was a stick, no, rather a Shepherd's Hook. Someone was holding it. It was Drew! Drew was in this good place, happy and content. *How nice*, she thought before the gentle baas became urgent.

Bess opened her eyes; the conscious part of her brain realizing the noise was coming from the monitor. The guardian in her became alert, taking seconds to orient herself.

She looked over to where James' head lay on the pillow beside her, his breathing heavy and methodical. She reached over and touched his face, making sure this was not the dream. His lips smiled, an involuntary act of appreciation.

Another baaa broke her connection to James, the noise louder, more urgent. The pain and fear in this call jerked Bess from her selfish pleasure. She slid from under the covers, standing on the oriental rug beside the bed, her naked body protected from chill by the heat from the bedroom's gas fireplace.

Bess picked up the monitor, pressing it to her ear, hearing the next urgent call for help. She reacted automatically, dressing in the change of clothes James had retrieved from her car. Taking the monitor with her, she walked down the stairs, never looking back. The shepherd was coming.

James awoke to find Sadie sitting on the end of the bed, stroking Millie, staring at the fireplace in the bedroom. He checked to make sure he was covered and pulled the quilt up to his shoulders. "Hey there," he said. "This is a surprise."

"Why do you have a fiwaplace in a bedwoom?" Sadie asked.

"Good question," James admitted. "The builder suggested it. Said it would be nice and cut costs on heating."

"So it saves money?" Sadie asked.

"I think it's more about being nice," James admitted.

The kitten crawled over to James, making her way to his face. Millie licked his nose and quickly returned to Sadie. "My kitty knows hews mine," Sadie announced proudly. "I wuvvs her and hews loves me."

"I'm glad," James said while looking around the bedroom. "Who sent you up here?"

"Miss Ginny said to get you. She's in the bawn hewping my mom. You must be vewy tiwed. Was you wowking wate?" Sadie asked.

"You go downstairs and I'll get dressed," James suggested. "I need to get a move on."

Sadie slipped off the bed, then turned to look back and ask, "Mista James, what cowa awe you gonna paint my mom?"

James was dumbfounded. He studied the little girl. Sadie stood very still, her arms cradling her kitten, her expression of concern visible in the glow from the fireplace. The scene reminded him of Bess, walking through the field, her arms cradling all the kittens wrapped in Sadie's pink coat. A lump rose in his throat.

"Don't use paint that sticks to hews," Sadie suggested. "I wike my mama the cowa hews is now."

"Good idea," James said.

Sadie heard him laughing as she walked down the steps. *He must like mornings*, she decided.

"He's coming," Sadie yelled as she ran into the barn. "He has a fiwaplace in his bedwoom!"

"He's never turned it on. It's the same reason he hasn't painted the outside of the house. He's waiting for *the one* to show up," Ginny said disgusted. "What a waste."

"It was buwning," Sadie said. "The fiwa was nice."

Ginny stopped what she was doing and turned to look at Bess, who blushed. "It's about time," Ginny announced.

"He says it saves money," Sadie reported. "He must need money."

"He needs lots of things," Ginny said laughing. "Hope he used his tub."

"Doesn't he wash?" Sadie asked, horrified.

"Usually just showers," Ginny said, realizing Bess didn't appreciate her teasing. "I think I better go make breakfast. How long before you two can join us?"

"We might not stay for breakfast," Bess said, obviously uncomfortable.

"Bess, I'd never forgive myself if you didn't stay. Please know that," Ginny said before walking out the door.

"Today Mama and me awe gonna take pictuwes of Wascal, all the kittens, Dipsy, and you," Sadie announced after drinking down the last of her milk.

Bess looked over at James and explained, "Then we need to leave. We need to get the pictures developed and get back to our own life."

"Mama, not wight away. I want to hewp Mista James miwk the goats." Sadie's fervent pleas touched a soft spot in Bess. She realized they both wanted to stay.

"Maybe for a little while. Mister James, would you take her picture when she milks Dipsy," Bess asked, looking into his blue eyes.

"Be glad to," he said, as a smile curved his lips. "Anything for you."

Ginny saw Bess look away, almost ready to bolt. "What can we do to make their milk taste better?" Ginny asked, in an attempt to keep her sitting.

Bess looked at the door, then over at Ginny. She took in a deep breath and suggested, "There are some simple tricks. You have to make sure everything is clean in the milking process. The milking equipment should be washed daily in the dishwasher or wash them with bleach and let them air dry."

Bess looked over at James and saw he was intently listening. She continued, "Wipe off the goat's udders before you milk. I kept a jar filled with water and grapefruit-seed extract in the barn. I'd wet down a clean washrag and use it to disinfect the udders. Never shoot the first squirt of milk in the pail. It carries bacteria. Put it in a cup, and throw it out far from where you milk."

"I better take notes," James said, as he stood and walked to his desk.

"Is it worth it?" Ginny said. "All this milking and all this preparation?"

"A goat is the poor man's cow," Bess said, relaxing and sipping more of her coffee. "Goats are like chickens and roosters. It's just part of having a small farm and the thrill of having everything you need. Besides, if you get the milk tasting right, you can make more than just soap out of goat milk. You can make cheese."

"Why would you make soap out of goat milk?" Ginny asked stunned.

"You haven't lived till you've used pure, natural goat soap, and it's not hard to make. The only thing I added was fresh herbs. I never used chemicals. All those expensive brands in the bottles are polluted with chemicals to make them last. The chemicals dry out your hair and skin. One cake of goat soap corrects all the damage they've done. It moisturizes as it cleans. You won't believe how it changes the texture of your skin and hair. Best shampoo you'll ever try."

"You wash your hair with a cake of soap?" Ginny asked amazed.

"Feew my haiw, Miss Ginny," Sadie suggested. "I use Mama's soap."

Ginny ran her fingers through Sadie's soft, blonde hair. "I'll be," she murmured.

"What do I do after I milk?" James asked, as he sat down and scribbled notes.

"Take the milk into the house and strain it through a disposable milk filter into clean, glass jars. Then put the milk into the freezer for at least two hours. The quick chilling will stop the enzyme activity without taking away the benefits of raw milk. You have to use raw milk to make some forms of cheese," Bess explained.

"Then it will be drinkable?" Ginny asked, still doubtful.

"It will taste wonderful, almost like cow milk. I like it better. If you added some sweet protein feed to their diet, you'd be amazed at the taste. The feed has a little molasses in it. Both you and the goats would love it," she promised before standing.

"There are few more things, but I don't think you'd like them," Bess said.

"What?" James asked, intrigued.

"Some farmers keep the buck goats far away from the does. They say the bucks stink so much it can affect the taste of the doe's milk," Bess said, before raising one eyebrow.

"That's mean," James said. "The buck would be lost without the does." His look made it clear to all adults that they were talking in metaphors.

"He'd survive," Bess advised him, with a slight grin.

"You never did that, Mama," Sadie added, as she stood. "You said that would be awful to keep them apart. You said they need to stay together to be happy."

James watched as Bess' face blushed. "Sometimes they need to adjust," she said softly, as she looked down, "for everyone else's sake. If you want to stay awhile longer," Bess added looking up, "I'll go dock the new lambs' tails. I've got my elastrator pliers and some bands in my car. It won't take me long."

"I want to watch," Ginny said, "if it doesn't hurt the little lambs."

"No, it's just a special pliers that opens the thick rubber bands, then I slip it down onto the tail. When the band closes down, the lambs hardly feel it. The tails drop off from lack of blood in a week or two," Bess explained.

"Beats amputation," Ginny said, just before leaving.

James watched as the two women left together. Sadie was clearing the table like a little old lady. "I'll help, James said. "I'll put them in the dishwasher."

"I want to wive here," Sadie said casually. "I can do wots of things to hewp."

James froze. "It is a nice place to live," he said carefully.

"Good," Sadie announced. "I awready picked out my room. I want the one with the bed in it upstaiws by youws."

"Sadie," James said looking down at her. "We can't all have what we want. Everyone has to want the same thing."

"Wemembew," Sadie said looking up at him, pointing one finger, which now had a fingernail, painted bright pink, "Mama does one thing at a time. You just have to wait tiww its time fow hew to move to the next thing. I'm good at waiting."

"It sounds like I need to buy chickens," James added.

"My mama loves chickens, but she weally woved ouw wooster. He was beautiful, took hew weeks to pick him out," Sadie explained. "Besides, youw eggs don't taste like ouws did, and I can get youw eggs when I'm hewe."

The two women heard Sadie and James laughter waft out the open kitchen window. "They sure get along well, don't they?" Ginny said.

"I'm not his *one*," Bess said, sighing. "You need to know that, Ginny. I've told him that; I don't want to hurt anyone."

"Oh," Ginny answered, stopping to pet Shep. "That's a shame. You three would make a great family, have a good life together."

"I'll never get married again. It hurts too much when things go bad," Bess pledged.

"If you think I'm going to agree with you, you're very wrong. I don't care what pain you've experienced in the past," Ginny said, as she walked toward Bess' car.

Her reaction shocked Bess. Ginny seemed angry, her steps becoming stomps. "Ginny, what's wrong?" Bess asked, walking faster to keep pace.

"I'm the wrong woman to say that to," Ginny said, her hands balling into fists.

"What do you mean?" Bess asked.

Ginny stopped and stared at Bess, her eyes wide. "I'm engaged to a Special Forces soldier. He's over there fighting his ass off to keep us safe. I got an email from his commander's wife, telling all of us to hold them in our prayers. That means he's in a firefight. I'm planning a wedding for a man who might not come home, but Mike's worth any pain I have to endure," Ginny said.

Bess reached out and hugged Ginny. "I'm so sorry. I've been so caught up in my own world that I forgot what you must be going through."

Ginny hugged her back, apologizing, "Boy, that felt good. I sure needed to yell at someone. I'm so damn mad. He's supposed to be on his way home. It must be something big for them to send him back into battle," Ginny said, suddenly crying.

The two women walked together into the meadow. Few words had been spoken. "I'm glad you came with me," Bess finally admitted. "I don't know if you're a religious person, but standing in a herd of sheep is the best way to see the bible come to life."

"I'm more spiritual than religious, but I've read the bible," Ginny admitted. "What do you mean?"

"The bible was written in shepherd's terms. Almost everyone in it had sheep, including Jesus. When you watch the sheep, you see bible verses coming to life and remember how he laid down his life to protect his flock," Bess explained. "We are his flock; I'm always comforted by that."

Two hours later, James walked up to Bess. She was spraying small dots of yellow on some of the sheep. "Why are you spraying my beautiful sheep?" he asked

"Hi, James," she said standing. "I promised to mark the ones that will go to the butcher right after they lamb."

"Here I wanted to thank you for comforting Ginny. She told me how you gave her hope. Something about shepherds protecting their flock?" James said looking puzzled.

"This is the hardest part of protecting your flock," Bess explained. "Look, this sheep has an overbite. Her lambs will probably carry that trait. If so, they all have to go."

"I don't care if they're not perfect," James admitted.

"You have to weed out the weak to keep the strong," Bess explained. "Besides, you have to use the meat for nourishment. If you don't use it, soon they'd be no reason to have sheep. You can't justify keeping all your sheep for fleece."

James turned and looked around his flock. "You've been busy. How many are going be slaughtered?" he asked.

"Only thirty," Bess said. "So far."

"What would I do with all that meat?" he asked.

"Why do you think lamb is the traditional meal for Easter?" Bess asked, as she patted the ewe on the rump and it took off.

"No idea. We always eat ham," James said, watching it sprint back to the flock.

"Because lambs are born in the spring. There are so many of them," Bess said. "Besides, your company can eat enough lamb so that you'd never have to sell any."

"It doesn't bother you?" James said. "You don't have a problem sending them off to be butchered?"

"I was raised on a farm," Bess said. "It's just the way it is. All 4-H kids learn that."

"You can decide that quickly," James said.

"Yup," Bess said. "I've learned to be practical and make decisions quickly."

"Bess," James said gently. "You don't have to decide anything about us that quickly. We can enjoy what we have together without any big decisions."

"If we spend a lot of time together, Sadie might get her hopes up about our relationship," Bess said.

"Sadie's already decided she wants to live here. Told me she wants the bedroom with the bed already in it. I told her we don't get what we want all the time. That everyone would need to make that decision. She seemed to understand that. Bess, I would hope that we'd always be able to stay friends, even if we don't stay romantically involved," James suggested.

"Do people do that?" Bess asked. "Do they stay friends if they break up?"

"Some do. I even know married couples who've divorced and are still the best of friends," James explained.

"I can't imagine," Bess admitted. "I've lived a very sheltered life."

"It's a new day," James promised. "We can always stay friends. Besides, you know more about farming than anyone else I've ever met, even Mitchell. I need you in my life."

"It is nice to be needed," Bess admitted. "I enjoy being here on your farm. I know things about the farm but not a lot about life off the farm. You could help me with that."

"I'd like nothing more," James answered. He paused and added, "Sadie says you can help me pick out a handsome rooster and some chickens. She says my eggs don't taste very good."

"I'd love to help you pick out a rooster and chickens," Bess admitted growing excited. "Your eggs do taste old."

"I can't eat old eggs," James decided, "but let me get the chicken coop built first."

"The Amish sell chicken coops at the Thomasville Flea market. I've checked them over. They're perfect and not expensive," Bess explained.

James reached out and put his arms gently around her, whispering, "There are other things you need to see too. You haven't seen my tree house yet."

"That's right," she whispered, as she looked at the magical structure over his shoulder. "I have to go up in that tree house sometime."

James started to laugh and Bess asked, "What's so funny?"

"Sadie made me promise not to use sticky paint on you. She likes the color you are now," James related.

They turned in time to see Ginny in the field, taking pictures of Sadie and Rascal, who was loudly braying.

Fifteen

"I'd like to share something with all of you," Bess explained at the Monday meeting. "Most of you know that Sadie just started talking again. What I haven't told you is why she stopped." Bess watched as all the former smiles faded on her coworker's faces. "I just found out that Sadie doesn't talk in school yet, but today she's planning to stand before her class and tell them what happened to make her stop talking. If she can do that, I should be able to tell you why."

Bess looked down at her hands and took in a deep breath. She then explained how her husband had died. When she looked up, most had tears in their eyes.

"Thank you for not prying. Both of us didn't have the words before now," Bess added and shrugged. "I had a dream the other night. Drew was in a field surrounded by our sheep and he was happy. I think he was telling me that it's time for us to move forward. Telling you how he died is a step in that direction."

"Does Sadie's teacher know what she plans to do today?" Trudy asked, obviously concerned.

"I took Sadie to school and talked to her teacher. She promised to call me around 11:15 and let me know how Sadie is doing.

I'm a nervous wreck, but Sadie seemed very calm and determined this morning. She's got pictures of her new kitten and some other farm animals to show her class," Bess explained.

Bess placed her hands on the table and rubbed her fingertips over the waxed, oak surface. "Thank goodness I'm going to teach the makeup spinning class today. It'll make the time go faster and the two women both know the full story. They were with me when Sadie and I finally started talking about it," Bess explained. "The day at the sheep farm brought it all back to us." She stood up and added, "I'll let you know when I get the phone call from Sadie's school. Thanks for caring."

The first section of the spinning lesson was spent washing raw fleece from The Funny Farm. Bess took advantage of the warm weather and spread one out on the grass. "Very few spinners are as lucky as you two. You've known all these animals, some you've even sheared. That is an amazing connection to the fiber that you'll be spinning," Bess said, as she sat down on the grass next to the fleece.

"Spinning is an art form that not only connects you to the sheep but also to generations of women throughout the world who've taken raw fiber and spun it to make fabric. It's truly a common thread that binds us to them," Bess said, touching the fleece. "Today we'll learn to wash the fleece, then to dye it a variety of colors. We'll use wool carders to comb all the fibers in the same direction to make what we spinners call roving. You're ready to spin once you have roving. Can you imagine knitting the yarn you created from this fleece into a sweater or scarf? Every time you slip it on, you'll remember sitting here today, beginning this journey. It never gets old, that feeling of connection to the earth and the sheep we all know."

Ginny and Fran's hands caressed the fleece, as if it was still part of a living creature.

"We only discard the outer edges of stained and matted wool. The rest will get submerged into a bucket with very hot water and some Dawn soap," Bess explained as she began ripping off the useless edges.

"Won't the wool shrink or get felted if you put it in hot water?" Ginny asked.

"No, not if you don't agitate it. It's the agitation that felts wool. You must have hot water to clean it. We'll let it sit in the hot, soapy water for about ten minutes. The hot water will loosen the lanolin and dirt so it can be drained off," Bess explained. "I have printed off detailed instructions for you to use at home."

Once the fleece had been cleaned, Bess placed a dye pot on an electric burner on a table outside. "This is the most exciting part," Bess said. "We're going to kettle dye this fleece. I've picked three colors: green, burgundy, and navy. I've prepared each of the dyes in jars by adding some vinegar and water. I'm putting more vinegar into the pot of water to open the fibers so it will accept the dye. We lower the wool into the hot water. Fran, you can push it down slowly with the potato masher." The women watched as it finally stayed below the water's surface.

"Now I'll just pour in the colors in three different areas of the pot. The dye will float down through the water and mix in areas they touch together. We'll get many shades of these colors, some from the colors mixing and some from different amounts of dye saturating into the fibers," Bess said as she continued.

By eleven o'clock, they'd spread the brightly dyed fiber onto a screen under a tree. "I love this part," Ginny admitted, "and just think. I can go home and dye as many fleece as I want. I've got access to a barn full."

"Let's go wash our hands," Bess suggested. "It's almost time for Sadie's teacher to call. Besides, we're going to get you started on your wheels now. I want you to use some roving I've already prepared before your work with this. It will be easier to learn with."

Bess answered the phone with an anxious, "How is Sadie?" She closed her eyes and listened intently.

"Sadie did a wonderful job, kept it short without too many details," the teacher reported. "She warned them it was a scary story but it had a happy ending. She told them about her dad's spirit being in the car with her helping her beep the horn. Is that all true?" the teacher asked. "Did she save your life?"

"Yes, Sadie absolutely saved my life, and she was only four. Drew had to be there with her," Bess explained.

"I've taught for over twenty years," the teacher revealed. "Sadie's story, and the way she told it, will be my most precious memory."

"Thank you for letting her tell it her way. How is Sadie?" Bess inquired.

"Thank you for giving me a head's up," the teacher said. "She's been smiling and talking all morning. The other kids are being very supportive. We posted the pictures of the animals up on the bulletin board."

As Bess hung up the phone, she realized she'd been shaking. *Too fast,* she thought. *Everything is going too fast.* Bess walked out the front door of the studio and headed down the road. The kittens ran out from the barn. Bess stopped, bent over, patted one, and thought of Cricket. *That's when this whirlwind started,"* Bess realized. *It was simpler back then. I'm not ready for so much changing.*

Bess noticed one independent kitten playing off by herself with a tuft of the fleece they had thrown out. The little cat tossed the bit of fiber into the air, caught it, and rolled around in delight. *Sadie's like that kitten; she's ready to strike out on her own and find happiness. I can't slow her down,* Bess realized, as she heard her friends walk out the front door eager to give support if needed.

Bess tucked Sadie into bed and sat down to listen to her prayers. They were different tonight, more conversation than prayer. Sadie said, "Thanks God. I had a gweat day. Pwease, teww Daddy I'm okay and so is Mom. He's in the fiewd with your sheep. I wove you, God, and I wove him."

Bess kissed her forehead and tucked her in. "I love you," Bess said, before standing to leave. Exhausted by the events of the day, Sadie was asleep before Bess closed her door.

Bess walked into the living room and sat down on the sofa. She picked up her knitting, lifting the fabric to her nose. She could still smell the wonderful aroma of lanolin and natural fiber. Lifting her legs and lying down, she closed her eyes and pictured the sheep in James' meadow; and then she fell sound asleep.

Bess was stroking one ewe and then her dream shifted. She was no longer with the sheep in the meadow. She was climbing up brightly colored steps in a tree. The leaves were all around her, rustling in anticipation, the breeze blowing against her face. She could see the door, painted cascading colors. It was wet, all the colors sticking to her hands, getting all over her. She tried to whip them off, but they smeared, soaking into her skin. Her hands were too wet now. She couldn't hold on. She grabbed a branch and hung on for dear life. The tree was hundreds of feet above the meadow. She heard someone calling. It was Sadie. Sadie was down in the meadow with the sheep. Who was with her? It was Drew. Sadie and Drew were together with the sheep far away. Sadie was screaming, "I don't wike those cowors. I wike Mom the way she was!"

The phone rang, jerking Bess back to reality. She was grateful, hating what the dream had become. On the third ring, she lifted the receiver still foggy. "Hello," she said, almost breathless.

"Hello," James said, his voice deeper than she remembered. "Are you all right? You sound winded."

"I fell asleep on the couch," Bess admitted.

"I'm sorry I disturbed you," James apologized.

"I'm not. I was having a nightmare. I had wet paint all over me, and Sadie hated the colors," Bess explained.

"That's odd," James said. "I'm up in the tree house painting." Quiet filled the airwaves. "Bess, Sadie wouldn't hate this picture. She'd like it very much."

"So much is happening too fast," Bess said, sitting on the wooden chair at the kitchen table, "but Sadie welcomes all the changes. She did a great job in school, seems much happier now. She talked all night about the different kids she got to know. She's becoming a regular chatter box."

"That's good," James suggested.

"I guess so, but I don't know," Bess admitted.

"I get it," James suggested. "When we were stationed on the outpost, we were isolated. We depended on only each other. We knew what everyone was feeling without needing words. You know, if they were hot, thirsty, scared, mad, hungry, bored, frustrated, or whatever. We were like one person after a while."

"That's what Sadie and I were like. I knew everything she was thinking," Bess admitted.

"When we came back to base, it was weird. The guys would call their families, get their heads thinking back to the life at home. They'd be thinking about things I'd never know. I lost control over them and I worried more," James explained. "I worried they might get some bad news and I wouldn't know. A guy can go crazy if he gets bad news at the wrong time," James explained.

"And you were still in charge. You had to keep them in line," Bess answered.

"It took me a while to learn that once we got back to base, I had to give them breathing room. I had to separate from them and give them space, trust them to handle whatever they came across," James said. "It's hard to let go."

"I don't want to let go," Bess admitted. "I'm not ready yet."

"I don't think mom's are supposed to let go," James said. "She's just a little girl; she needs you. She's going to explore this big, wide world, and you have to help her."

"Truth is," Bess admitted. "I'm not much of an explorer. I like things to stay the same. I feel safer when they do."

"I hear you," James answered, "but I have a suggestion and some good news."

"I like good news."

"I sold a painting tonight," James informed her. "It was hanging in a gallery in Baltimore. Matter of fact, the buyer asked the gallery owner if I had more paintings of sheep."

Bess laughed and it felt wonderful. Finally she asked, "How many do you have on hand?"

"I'm down to just fifteen. I keep them stored in that building that looks like a garage. Some people park their cars, I park my paintings," James chuckled. "I keep pictures of each of them on my computer. I sent them to the buyer, and he wants me to bring three more to his Inn."

"He must love sheep," Bess suggested.

"He likes to hang them in his guest rooms. The guy owns a big bed and breakfast in Maryland. Invited me to spend the night. Want to come with me?" James asked.

"I don't know," Bess said taken back. "What about Sadie?"

"You'd have to work that out. I promise it wouldn't become a regular thing. I won't ask you to leave Sadie behind very often. Please know that," James said.

"How long would we be gone?" Bess asked.

"We could go for one or two nights," James said, "whatever you felt comfortable with. I'd like to show you around Maryland. Have you ever been in a big city?"

"No, never," Bess admitted.

"We could explore and make a list of places to take Sadie in the future. Truth is, Baltimore is not more than an hour away from us," James explained.

"What's a bed and breakfast like?" Bess asked. "I've never stayed at one."

"They're usually in a home with several rented-out rooms. They provide breakfast to the lodgers. A married couple whose last name is Shepherd owns this one. The name of their place is The Shepherds' Inn and that's why they want all the guestrooms to have pictures of sheep. They're expanding their place by adding cottages. We'd be staying in a cottage," James explained.

"I'd feel better staying in a cottage. I might sound ridiculous, but I'd be embarrassed staying with a couple when we're not married. Silly, Huh?" Bess said

"No, I understand. You've been married most of your life. I'm sure all of this is very new to you. Is it too soon for you to go away with me?" James asked.

"No, I think it comes at a good time. The ewes won't have any babies for a few more weeks," Bess reasoned. "Once they start, you won't be able to leave. After that you'll be busy with all the lambs and deciding which stay and which go. This is the only break you'll get for months," Bess reasoned. "Who'll milk the goats?"

James laughed and then stated, "You're the only woman I know who would worry about that. Do you know how adorable you are? How much I want to hold you in my arms?"

"James, I'm like a duck out of water. I'm not really ready for all of this," Bess admitted.

"Yes you are," James said. "Sadie's a chip off the old block. Her mom's a take-charge woman who can handle just about anything. Let's go exploring together."

"Exploring," Bess said. "I can't think of anyone I'd rather go exploring with than you. I'll call Fran and ask if she would like to have Sadie spend Friday and Saturday night. She does like to watch lacrosse."

"Tell Fran that we'll take Judy with us to Baltimore to the Aquarium sometime soon," James suggested. "Sadie would probably like to have her along."

"There's an Aquarium in Baltimore?" Bess asked.

"There's a whole world you haven't seen yet," James said. "You teach me about my sheep; I'll show you the world."

Sixteen

"Thanks for picking Sadie up," Bess said. "She's been excited ever since I told her about spending the weekend at your house."

"So has Judy," Fran explained. "They really enjoy each other. Now you have a wonderful time."

"We're driving down to Maryland and having dinner with the Shepherd Family," Bess explained. "The wife is cooking dinner. I'm thinking of giving her this; what do you think?" Bess asked, as she lifted a needle-felted sheep from a gift bag.

"It's beautiful, but you shouldn't buy anything for her. How could you part with this sheep? Look at those big, loving eyes," Fran added, as she studied the eight-inch wool animal.

"I made it from some of James' fleece. I'm glad you like it, because I made that one for you. This is the one for the Inn owners," Bess said, as she lifted one from another bag.

"They're amazing! They each have their own personality," Fran exclaimed.

"I know. It just happens once you start making them. Wool is the easiest material to sculpt with. It takes on its own shape, and I'm always amazed how they turn out," Bess admitted. "If you'd like to learn how to make them, I can show you and Ginny. I teach classes at the shop, but you could learn at James' farm while the kids have fun playing together."

"Promise?" Fran asked. "Can I make a wool kitten?"

"Absolutely. Look on my mantel. I've made one of Cricket and her kittens. Look, here's Millie, Callie and Junior," Bess said, lifting the three.

Fran lifted them and studied the sculptures. "They're so true to life." Then she smiled adding, "I notice you only made your three kittens."

Bess studied the little group of animals. "I wonder why?" Bess said. "I should add your two kittens."

"Bess, you don't need to. These are the kittens in your immediate family," Fran suggested.

"No, this one belongs to James" Bess said, lifting the little, black kitten with her fingers.

Fran looked over at Bess, shrugged, smiled, and added, "They do their own thing while you make them. I think this little group is destined to stay together."

"I don't know," Bess admitted, looking into Fran's eyes. "James promised that we'll always be friends, even if it doesn't work out for us romantically."

"Why wouldn't it work out for you romantically?" Fran asked. "He's handsome, kind, smart, and he's a shepherd. What's not to work out?"

"I know, James is almost perfect," Bess admitted. "That's just the point. I have flaws and Sadie comes first in my life. I get caught up in one thing at a time. I'm not neat, never went to college, grew up in a small town, and don't know a thing about the city life. We're too different," Bess explained.

"You think James is perfect?" Fran asked, while laughing. "You two must be made for each other. I wouldn't put up with his crazy lifestyle no matter how good looking he was."

"What crazy lifestyle?" Bess asked.

"See," Fran said. "You think it's perfectly normal to have all those animals who need all that care. You two deserve each other."

Bess spent the next half hour packing and changing her clothes. She decided to wear a dress, since James said he'd wear a sports coat. She lifted a spinach green, jersey frock off the hanger and slipped the soft fabric over her head. It slid down easily. Bess stepped into her black heels, and then put on red lipstick, eye shadow, and green turquoise earrings. After fluffing up her hair, she turned to accomplish her next chore, without even checking her appearance.

James studied the little house at the end of the driveway. It sat on a patch of grass with one large tree. A porch swing hung on the small, front porch. Two plaid, woven pillows and a hand-knit blanket rested on the swing. A pot of pansies sat on each of the three front steps. James knew he had found Bess and Sadie's home.

He pulled into the driveway and noticed a movement in the window. He looked and his heartbeat jumped. Bess was standing at the window, looking out at him. Her hand lifted and she waved, her face radiant and welcoming. He gripped the steering wheel to steady himself. His eyes memorized each detail, the glow of the stained-glass chandelier behind her, the hand-crocheted curtains, the red-haired woman, her beautiful red lips turned up in a smile, the dots of green on her earlobes, and the smooth, emerald dress clinging to her full breasts and trim body.

He had dreamed of just such a scene in the desert where he thought he was destined to die. In his dream, the woman didn't have a face or vibrant colors or a loving nature. She'd just been an illusion. Bess was real, alive, and waiting for him. He couldn't move, not yet. He needed time to calm his emotions and regain control of his body's reaction to seeing her. He took in a deep breath and watched as she turned, flipped off the lights, and walked out the door.

James got out of the car and met her on the front porch apologizing, "I was coming inside to help you. I just needed a few minutes."

Bess looked up into his eyes, sat her suitcase down and walked into his arms. They stood together embracing on the front porch, grateful she had turned off the porch light. He kissed the top of her head, smelled the scent of her shampoo. "I've missed you," he whispered.

"I've missed you too," Bess admitted, as she lifted her lips to gently kiss his. Her arms encircled his neck, noticing he wore a camel suit jacket, a blue shirt, and green tie. "We match," she whispered, referring to their colors.

"We match perfectly," he said, as he thought how well their bodies fit together. "Bess, I don't want to share you with these strangers. You look so beautiful in that green dress."

"Just remember, you get to take this dress off, once we're in our own cabin," Bess promised, nuzzling her cheek against him.

"Let's hope they don't plan on a long night," James suggested, as they held hands and walked down the steps. "Have everything you need?"

"Everything I need," Bess said, squeezing his hand.

"I can't decide," Marie Shepherd announced. "I think we need all three."

"I was thinking the same thing," Tim Shepherd admitted, "but I'd like this one hung over our fireplace." Tim lifted the largest painting of a fluffy, white ewe and her three baby lambs.

"That's my latest painting; I'm glad you like it. It seems our ewes are now having three lambs," James said, smiling over at Bess.

"So you have your own sheep?" Marie asked, sitting next to Bess on the sofa.

"Too many, I've been thinking," James admitted. "Bess tells me we could have over six hundred by the end of lambing season."

"Oh my," Marie said blinking. "That's a lot of sheep. I always thought this place needed some sheep."

"Well, I brought one for you," Bess said, handing the gift bag to Marie. "We appreciate you inviting us to your Inn."

Marie lifted the needle-felted sheep out of the bag, her eyes growing wide. "This is magnificent. Is this really for me?" she asked turning to Bess. "I love it."

"Thank you, I made it from The Funny Farm's wool," Bess explained. "It's needle-felted."

"It's magical," Marie said, as both James and Tim walked over to see it.

"How did you make that?" James asked. "It is wonderful."

"Don't you know?" Marie asked, "or do you paint and take care of your sheep while your wife takes care of the house and makes these?"

Bess' face blushed as she admitted, "We're not married."

"Oh," Marie said, shaking her head in embarrassment. "I saw your wedding ring."

Bess looked down at her hand and stared at the simple gold band. She looked up at Marie and explained, "I'm a widow."

"For how long?" Marie asked, as the men turned away and walked out to refresh their drinks.

"Over two years," Bess admitted.

"I'm sorry. You seem to have found a good friend," Marie suggested.

"I have," Bess said. "I have a daughter," she confessed, without knowing why.

"How lucky. I love my kids," Marie assured her. "Has James met her?"

Bess explained the story of how they met, the men coming in to hear the end of the tale. "What a wonderful way to meet someone. Does Sadie like The Funny Farm?" Marie asked.

"She loves it. There's a baby donkey that only likes Sadie. They're inseparable," Bess said happily.

"Come help me in the kitchen," Marie said standing. "I think supper is ready."

Bess followed her into a large, semi-commercial kitchen. "You must cook for big groups of people," Bess said, staring at the large stove.

"I do and plan to do more. I'm going to offer an evening meal to my guests. I'm trying out a recipe on you. We're also thinking of adding a small store. Nowadays we have to take advantage of every way to make ends meet. It's hard to make an Inn this size profitable."

"What are you going to sell in the store?" Bess asked. "I can make homemade goat soap from James' goat milk and you could sell needle-felted sheep and other animals. If you wanted, you can sell my homespun yarn or knit scarves and sweaters. Would you be interested in any of those things?" Bess asked.

"Absolutely. Maybe we should only sell things made on a farm or from sheep," Marie said, forgetting about the food. "Would thirty percent be too much to ask for commission?"

"More than fair," Bess said. "I'm really excited. Would you consider having a ewe and her three lambs live here on your land? I couldn't help thinking as we drove up how beautiful they'd look in the pasture."

"I love that idea. Let's talk to Tim about it. I think we'll see a great deal more of you two," Marie said. "May I be bold and tell you something?"

"Of course," Bess answered.

"It's time to take that wedding ring off," Marie suggested.

Bess looked down and stared again at her ring. "I'd feel naked without it. I feel like it's part of me. Everything seems to be changing so fast."

"And that's a bad thing?" Marie asked. "I don't think your finger will be bare for long."

"I should focus on Sadie," Bess said stepping back.

"I've always believed that the happiest children have parents who love them and each other. Happy in means happy out. It's all a matter of perception, how you see the world around you. I've probably said too much," Marie apologized.

Bess watched as Marie lifted the casserole dish and walked into the dining room.

Something Marie had said reminded her of the Chief's own words. Singing Bird's father had said, "Take one step at a time until you're ready to see the happiness that surrounds you." *How could I have forgotten that?* Bess wondered. Alone, she tilted her head, placing her fingers around the ring and twisted it. The band moved easily; and after one tug, it was off her finger. Bess slipped the ring into the pocket of her dress, wiggling her naked finger with the white band of skin.

Bess picked up the bowl of salad and walked toward the happy, laughing voices in the dining room.

"How would we learn about taking care of sheep?" Marie asked. "I don't want to end up with six hundred."

"If you wanted to take one of our ewes and her three lambs, I'd be more than happy to give them to you. Without a ram, they wouldn't multiply," James assured her.

"Of course," Marie said laughing at herself. "You see how much I know about raising animals. Maybe it's too much for us," Marie admitted.

"The sheep could save time spent mowing. If you wanted to consider it," Bess added, "you could contact the local 4-H Sheep Club. They'd love to teach you how to care for your sheep. We can help shear them when it comes time. I can show you how to needle-felt animals from their fleece. You could sell your own creations in the store."

"My wife is quite the artist," Tim admitted. "She doesn't paint, but she gardens and does all our decorating."

The conversation went on for hours, and by desert they were recommending sites to see around their Inn. "You're that close to D.C.?" James said, his fork stopping mid air.

"Only forty-five minutes away," Tim explained. "It's an easy drive to Baltimore or Washington. That's one reason we bought this place. Didn't you tell me you were in the Special Forces?"

"Yes," James said, as he stared over the table at Tim.

"Arlington National Cemetery is only thirty minutes from here. Many of our repeat guests stay here when they go to visit friends or family. Some come once a month," he said, looking at James.

"I don't know where Mitchell's grave is," James admitted, turning to look at Bess. "I was still stationed on the outpost when they flew him home. I couldn't go to the funeral."

"We'll find it," Bess said. "We'll find it somehow."

"Come with me," Tim urged James. "I'll pull up the map of the National Cemetery. If you give me Mitchell's full name, we can print out a map to his gravesite."

"You're kind to offer to go with him," Marie said, as the men left. "It might be a difficult day."

"I knew Mitchell," Bess answered. "He was the 4-H leader at one of our camp retreats."

"Really?" Marie exclaimed. "Talk about destiny."

"I don't know if it's destiny; anybody with sheep in Montana knew the other shepherds," Bess explained.

"Perhaps so," Marie answered, "but how many shepherds from Montana went into the Army special forces to serve in Afghanistan as James' second in command?"

"No one else," Bess whispered, as she turned to stare in the direction James had walked.

"I think fate had a lot to do with why you ended up staying at The Shepherd's Inn, thirty minutes from Mitchell's gravesite?" Marie added. "I think its got to be destiny, fate, or kismet when your life catapults in a new direction. You just have to be open to the world and let it happen."

"Really?" Bess asked, as she rubbed the newly naked finger on her left hand.

"That's what one guest on Oprah's show said," Marie added, "and we all know Oprah doesn't invite fools on her show."

Seventeen

"Nice people, but I couldn't wait to get you alone. How far is this cabin?" James asked.

Marie said it's beside the pond, the one with aqua shutters. There it is. It looks lovely," Bess exclaimed.

"I don't care what it looks like as long as it has a door that locks, a bathroom, and a big bed. Bess, you take my breath away. How did I ever get so lucky to find you?" James asked.

"According to Marie, it was destiny that brought us together," Bess said, reaching for his hand.

James turned to smile at her. "Bess, I'm in love with you. You know that, don't you?" James confessed, surprising himself.

Her hand rose to her heart, her lips parted but nothing came out. She whispered, "What about Sadie?"

"Sadie?" James said laughing, "that little girl had me around her finger the first day we met. The other morning when I woke up and she was sitting on the end of my bed, I got a glimpse of what being a dad would be like. She was petting Millie and staring into the fire. I've never felt so important in my whole life."

"Is it too soon for us to be so in love?" Bess asked. "Is it possible for us to just know this is right?"

"Do you feel the same as I do?" James asked. "Are you saying you love me?"

"I tell you things I never told anyone, I respect you, I'm not afraid to disagree with you, you make me laugh, at night I dream about you, and I crave being with you. I mean it. I'm so drawn to you that when you come close, I can hardly breathe. Just holding your hand gives me goose bumps," Bess admitted.

They sat in the car, quiet surrounding them. "Will you marry me?" James asked.

Bess sat staring at the full moon and its perfect reflection in the pond. *One husband in heaven and one on earth? Could it be a sign?* Bess wondered. Being part Native American, she knew the answer. *Nature sends mankind signals every day.*

"Yes," Bess said. "I would love to spend my life finding happiness with you." She felt his fingers gently caress the newly bare, ring finger.

"I can hardly move," James confessed. "I want to remember every second of this moment. The cottage looks like a perfect love nest, with spring violets blooming in the grass. Right here, you said you'd marry me. You just made me the happiest man in the world. I can't believe I'm so blessed. I don't deserve you."

"You deserve to have a life full of love and joy. So do I. It is destiny," Bess said.

"I've killed men," James admitted. "I've done terrible things in my life."

"Whatever you did was for the love of your country. You were a hero," Bess said gently.

"I've made mistakes. I zigged when I should have zagged," James admitted. "That's what Mitchell and I used to say when we messed up. I didn't have to go on patrol that day. I had a feeling we were going to be ambushed. I was arrogant enough to believe we could handle anything. Men died because of that."

"Did men live because you were in charge?" Bess asked.

James turned to look at her. "Yes, some lived because of me. My God, I love you," he muttered.

He got out of the car and walked up the steps of the cottage. He opened the front door and returned to the car for Bess. She waited, watching him as he moved. He opened the car door and reached for her hand. She stood up and walked into his arms, hugging him, and kissing his neck. He reached down and lifted her into his arms. "Tonight is the first day of the rest of our lives," he whispered as he carried her up the steps and across the threshold.

He gently lowered her to a standing position and turned to flip on the lights. They both stood wide-eyed as they looked around the cozy quarters. Chintz fabric, with tiny cabbage roses, flowed over the bedspread, chairs and drapes. The shiny, cotton fabric made the flowers look fresh, almost fragrant. The furniture was painted a soft shade of aqua, the walls a pale yellow, the deep, brown, pine flooring grounding the room.

Tim must have slipped out long enough to surprise them by hanging one of James' pictures. It was now centered over the bed, the sheep looking directly at them, almost smiling.

James took in a deep breath and suggested, "The bathroom is yours while I go get our things. Then I'm locking that door and keeping the world outside."

She stood barefoot in front of him, lifting her arms up as he slowly slipped her dress over her head. His clumsy motion revealed just how new this all was to him. His nervous cough underscored how carefully he was trying to be gentle. She smiled under the fabric, endeared by his behavior.

They both jumped as her wedding ring fell from the pocket in her dress, hitting the floor and rolling around until it stopped. Bess bent down and picked it up, carefully placing it on the dresser. She turned and walked back to James.

She had worn a black, silk slip and his expression displayed his fascination with the undergarment. His fingers caressed the fabric, touched the lace trim. "Is this a slip?" he asked.

"Yes, it comes off easily," Bess urged.

"I've never seen one," James admitted. "I like the way it feels."

Bess decided he needed prompting, so she began unbuttoning his shirt, and she watched as he closed his eyes and breathed heavily at her touch. Once unbuttoned, he shrugged it off, letting the shirt drop to the floor. Bess moved forward, and he felt the silk fabric of her slip rubbing against this chest. He groaned, saying, "I like that thing, love the feel of you in it."

Bess reached behind herself and undid her bra. She slipped it off, then stepped back and stepped out of her panties. All that remained was the black slip.

He followed her lead, undressing himself until he stood erect and naked. Bess walked forward and let his hands caress her, feeling the warmth of her naked body flow through the silk.

"Bess, how did I ever get so lucky?" he whispered. "I can't believe you're going to be my wife."

"I am all yours," Bess whispered. "Now and forever."

"Through thick and thin?" James asked as he kissed her head. "There will be rough times. Everyone has rough times."

"Through thick and thin," Bess promised, "with one deal breaker."

"Tell me so I don't do anything to lose you," James requested.

"Never say you don't want me anymore. I'd leave if you do," Bess admitted.

"I'll always want you, that I know," James said as he bent down to kiss her lips. "Always and forever."

Bess broke from his grasp and went to the bed. He watched as she turned down the bedcovers and slipped beneath the sheets. He studied her, as she smiled and reached up toward him, hesitating before flicking off the lights. She was so beautiful that he felt cheated when her vision slipped from his view. He hurried toward the bed and her waiting arms.

His lovemaking was almost reverent, showing deep and solemn respect. This was his betrothed, the woman he chose for life. She would bear his children, nurture his family, love him throughout it all. He was totally overwhelmed with the promise of their union. Everything about her seemed miraculous, the curve of her neck, scent from her hair, the supple texture of her skin and the toned muscles that lay beneath it. When she moaned in sexual reaction to his caress, he felt empowered as never before and became lost in the pursuit of an encore.

In the dark, his fingers traced each inch of her body, like a blind man reading Braille. He discovered her bellybutton was tucked in, her hip bones protruded with stomach flat between them. Her hands were small, yet strong and nimble. The feel of her breasts fascinated him. When he caressed them, she moaned. When he lowered his lips to kiss them, she cried out. When he sucked on their nipples, she dug her fingernails into his back. When he rubbed his cheek lightly against them, she moaned again.

Her legs were strong, pushing her body against him, nudging him with her groin. He lowered himself to kiss her there, loving the scent of her inner body. He explored her gently, finding new ways to make her sigh, whimper, and cry out in appreciation.

When he could hold back no longer, they united in both body and soul, the explosion destroying any doubts or concerns. They lay exhausted, happy, and still united as they fell into a deep, sound sleep.

At breakfast, they made the announcement. "We got engaged last night," James proclaimed, jubilant with the news.

The strangers around the table reacted with genuine joy. "How lovely," an older woman exclaimed. "I needed to hear wonderful news. Life does go on, doesn't it?" she said before returning to buttering her toast and her own sorrow.

"Are you visiting someone in Arlington Cemetery?" James asked, without thinking.

"My son," she said, looking up with tears. "He was only nineteen. He'll never get married," she whispered but all heard.

"You must be proud of him," Bess murmured.

"No, I'm mad at him. He didn't need to die. Certainly not like that," she said, still looking at her toast, "in some desert, blown to tiny pieces." She looked up and apologized. "I shouldn't be saying this out loud. I should be keeping it to myself."

"I feel the same way," another woman said from the end of the table. "My son was only twenty-two. He was engaged to be married, a lovely girl who's heartbroken. She'll go on, find another man to love, but I've lost my only child. I can't believe he's gone. I sit by his grave and stare at his name on the headstone, but that's not my son. Greg was tall with blonde hair and flashing brown eyes. He always hugged me and twirled me around; my feet would leave the ground. All I have left is a white headstone. I can't understand what happened. He was going to be a teacher, loved kids. Now he's gone, he's a name on that headstone."

Bess looked at the faces around the breakfast table. She guessed half were faces of bereaved, the others uncomfortable visitors. When she turned to look at James, she noticed he was pale, his jaw clenched to hold back his feelings.

"Do you come to visit often," a kind young man inquired.

"At least once a month. I can't seem to stay away. I sit and read, knit, or nap. It's like how I used to sit by his side when he was a little boy, sick in bed. I guess I'm just waiting for him to get better," she admitted. "He isn't, is he?"

"No," the other mother said sadly. "I just can't believe it."

"Maybe you shouldn't go so often," the young man's spouse suggested. "Your son would want you to get on with your life."

"Get on to what?" the mother asked. "Get on with my laundry, cooking, grocery shopping? I don't know what to get on with?"

"You said you knit," Bess said gently. "Would you consider knitting hats for charity. There's also a group that knits squares and then others sew them together to make blankets for charity. Maybe that would help?"

"I could do that," one mother admitted. "My church asks us to do those things. I must be good for something like that."

"Knitting isn't the answer," the other mother announced. "I want my son back." She stood up and walked out the front door, her napkin still in her hand.

"I should be going," the other mother said, standing. "My son is waiting." They all watched as she stood, folded her napkin, and laid it on the table. She nodded and departed slowly.

Marie walked out from the kitchen and sat down at the woman's place saying, "I apologize if this has started your day off badly. We're glad to provide a comfortable and safe environment for our grieving parents, but we want to make sure those of you who are

vacationing have a joyful experience. We're opening a small dining room for those who are mourning. We find people need to
talk to each other. In the future, we strive to make your mornings
more cheerful."

"Tell me," Marie said turning to Bess. "Did I hear you say that
you're engaged? I'm so happy for you two."

Upon leaving, Bess asked James, "Do you still want to go to the
cemetery?"

"More than ever," James said. "Why didn't I go before now? I
should've been visiting all the men who died under my command.
Instead, all I did was party with the living."

"James, I think the departed are with you when you all get
together. Don't you?" Bess asked, growing concerned.

"I don't know. I need to find out how it feels at the gravesite,"
James admitted. "I need to stop and buy a dark beer before we go.
I don't think I'll find Mitchell's favorite."

"Let me guess. He drank Montana's Moose Drool beer," Bess
said, trying to lighten the mood.

"I keep forgetting you knew him. Did you ever taste that beer?"
James asked.

"Of course, it's made by the Big Sky Brewing Company, in Montana. It's a malty beer, a deep, brown color. Love that taste," Bess
explained.

"You describe it to the beer distributor. Let's try to get as close
as we can. I don't want to disappoint Mitchell. We always promised
each other that we'd share a beer at the other's gravesite," James
explained. "I need to keep my promise."

"What is your favorite beer?" Bess asked, as they sat in the car
and began their trip.

"Rolling Rock; it's made in Pennsylvania," James said, smiling for the first time since breakfast.

"Are you going to be all right visiting Mitchell's grave site?" Bess asked.

"You want the truth?" James asked.

"Always. Let's try not to lie to each other," Bess suggested.

"I honestly don't know. I need to do this," James said. "I just know I need to do this."

"We'll do this together," Bess said, reaching for his hand. "I'm with you through *thick or thin*, remember?

Eighteen

Bess noticed the change in his decorum from the moment he spotted men in uniform. He strode stiff and straight; when not walking he spread his legs, placing his arm folded behind. His chin was higher, his cadence uniform and wide. He was more by himself than with her, more soldier than fiancé.

Bess read all the exhibits, studied all the plaques. James stood talking to a guide who marked a map to various grave sites. When James returned, she noticed the map had eight highlighted locations. She looked up into his eyes and recognized the glare of someone focused on just one thing. She understood his frame of mind.

Within an hour they located Mitchell's grave. In that time, they had heard the sound of a twenty-one gun salute and taps. The atmosphere was one of both grief and national pride.

Bess spread out a blanket and sat at Mitchell's gravesite. She watched James as he inspected the spot, reading the stone, brushing off its top, checking the grass and finally settling into the significance of the place.

He chose to stand, feet apart, staring down at the grass, guarding it from something unseen. He stayed in that position for over an hour, only the repeated chorus of ceremonial shots, bugles, or rolling caisson drew his focus temporarily away.

The beer lay on the blanket, unopened and ignored. Alerted by the mothers' discussion, Bess had suspected what may occur. She'd brought her knitting and sat respectfully working one row after another. It passed the time and eased the strain. She also looked around their immediate area. People sat on chairs, one lay on the grass beside the tombstone, some read books, while others drank a beer talking to their departed.

Bess grew comfortable with the setting. She placed her knitting on the blanket and sat crossed legged saying out loud, "Mitchell, I still remember everything you taught me about sheep. You were right, they can be determined things. I use that whistle you taught us to get their attention. My daughter thinks I use it too much to call her," Bess said laughing.

"If you look around, you might find Drew. He's up there in heaven, probably with a flock of sheep. Please tell him Sadie and I are doing all right. I'm in love with a great man," Bess said, looking up at James.

"I don't think Mitchell needs to hear about all that," James said, annoyance on his face.

"What should he hear?" Bess asked. "Would you like to toast a beer?" She extended her hand holding the bottle.

"No, I'm not in the mood," James said, growing still and quiet again.

Bess picked up her knitting and began working again. The minutes slipped past slowly, her heart heavy with the emotions radiating from James. She looked up at him, saw his tears and knew he was far away, back on the foreign soil where Mitchell had died. Only the sound of his cell phone broke the quiet. He jumped when it rang, pulled it from his pocket as if he wanted to throw it, until his eyes identified the sender.

"It's Ginny," James announced, as he gave it to Bess. "Would you talk to her, please. I'm not in the mood."

Bess reached up and took the phone, grateful that it was ready for her to speak, "Hello," she said toward the thing.

"Bess is that you?" Ginny asked, her voice sounding emotional.

"Yes, Ginny are you all right?"

"No. Can you come home? I need James home," Ginny admitted.

"What's happened?" Bess asked, as she stood.

"I received another email. It's Mike. He's in the battle that's on the news. I don't know what to do! Bess, are you two on your way home?" Ginny rambled.

"James, talk to Ginny. Mike is in the battle that's on the news," Bess said, pushing the phone toward him.

"Ginny, Mike is going to be all right. He's as tough as they come," James said, as he raked his hand through his hair. "Where is he? Do you know?"

Bess watched as he listened to his sister, his body language expressing his dire concern. "We'll be home in a few hours." he said as he motioned to Bess to get ready to leave.

James reached down and grabbed two beers. He popped open the tops of both and took one sip from each bottle. "A hell of a way to share a beer," he said as he poured them onto the gravesite. "I have to go. Seems Mike, that dumb son of a bitch, has got himself in a pile of shit. Ginny wants me home in case the call comes. I'll be back. I promise to come often," he said as he patted the gravestone. "I should have stayed in," he added surprising Bess.

"I belong over there. They need me over there." He turned and strode toward their car.

Bess walked behind him, amazed at how hard his feet hit the ground.

"Will you tell Marie that we can't spend the night?" James said, when they pulled up to the Inn Office. "I'll get our things out of the room."

Bess got out of the car and watched James speed toward their cottage. She shook her head before entering the office. "Marie, you're everywhere in this place, aren't you?" Bess said, trying to appear casual.

"Are you doing all right?" Marie asked.

"We got a call from James' sister. Her fiancé is in danger over in Afghanistan. We need to be with her in case a call comes," Bess explained.

"Of course," Marie said. "Please tell me that you're both coming back. We enjoyed our time with you."

"I hope so," Bess said honestly.

"Did you get my wedding ring?" Bess asked, as she slid in the car.

"What wedding ring?" James asked confused.

"The ring that fell out of my pocket. I put it on the dresser," Bess said.

"No, I forgot it. I left the key in the room," James explained.

"Wait here, I'll get another key from Marie," Bess asked, before jumping out of the car. They drove to the cottage, and Bess went in and found her ring. She slipped it on, as she had done so often over the years. She picked up both keys and took them with her. "I have to leave these keys off with Marie," Bess suggested.

"I see you found your ring," James said, as his eyes looked at her finger.

"Just habit," Bess said, trying to take it off

"You might lose it again. Just leave it on," James suggested, looking straight out the window.

"What's happening, James?" Bess asked.

"I should be over there, Bess," James decided.

"You did your time," Bess said. "It's not your job anymore."

"It could be," James explained. "The fighting is still going on. I should be with my brothers in arms."

"You should stay here with your arms around me," Bess said, looking at him before getting out of the car and returning the keys.

When she returned, she settled in for the ride. James had turned on the radio, a sign he didn't want to talk. Bess picked up her knitting and consoled herself that they'd be home soon and The Funny Farm would settle his mood.

Ginny met them at the door, tears streaming from her eyes. "I can't get any more information," she explained. "James, tell me what's going on now. I need to know."

"It's not easy to explain. A situation like this is more about waiting than about fighting. It's an adult snow ball fight. They lob things at you, you duck and lob things back. What sounds simple gets dangerous just because it can't be predicted. All you can do is react and that can drive a man crazy," James said walking to the refrigerator and grabbing a beer. "Politics say we can't attack. It's a bullshit way to fight a war."

"Can I get you one?" he asked Bess. "I bet you're hungry too. I was a terrible host this weekend."

"I'll make myself a sandwich. Want one?" Bess asked, as she opened the refrigerator.

"No, how about you, Sis? Did you eat anything?" James asked, as he sat beside Ginny.

"Of course. I ate two bags of Cheese Curls. Look, my fingers are permanently stained gold," Ginny said, lifting her fingers. "I'm so glad you two came home. I feel better when you're here. Why is Mike still over there? He should be packing to come home."

"They can keep him in as long as they need him," James reminded her. "He's got the specialized training they need. He's probably saving lots of kids' lives right now."

"I want him to save his own life," Ginny complained. "He's done his time."

James looked up at Bess and their eyes met for the first time since early in the morning. "I feel guilty as hell for not staying in," James explained. "I could be helping them over there."

"We had an unfortunate incident at the breakfast table this morning. Two mothers were grieving for their sons. When we went to visit Mitchell's gravesite, we saw others," Bess explained.

"You two spent your romantic getaway at Mitchell's gravesite?" Ginny asked. "Bro, are you blooming nuts?"

"I'm glad we did," James said, standing. "I should have gone a long time ago."

"This was your time with Bess," Ginny suggested. "You gave up time with Bess to visit Mitchell?"

"It just all seemed to happen," James said, shaking his head. "Everything happened too fast this weekend." He looked over at Bess and shrugged.

"So it seems. James, can you drive me home? I forgot something I need to take care of," Bess asked, as she took her last bite of her bologna sandwich.

"Of course," James agreed. "I'll be home in a half hour, Ginny. Call me if you need to talk."

"I owe you an apology," James said, as he turned the key and pulled the car out of the driveway.

"You owe me an explanation, not an apology," Bess demanded. "What's going on here? Are you lost between the future and the past?"

"I don't deserve a future," James announced, his jaw tight as he talked. "I have a responsibility to fulfill for my men. I'm a trained soldier, not a shepherd, and certainly not husband material."

"Or father material?" Bess said sadly. "Too many unknowns? You can't imagine what may happen in a life that's not reactive?"

"You're angry, I can see that," James acknowledged. "I deserve whatever you throw my way."

"I deserve the truth," Bess demanded. "You're afraid of commitment."

"Maybe I am," James admitted. "I have too much going on in my head to be a decent husband to you or a good father to Sadie. I'm still figuring out how to live without a gun on my hip."

"Do you love me or was that just the thing to say at the time?" Bess asked.

"I love everything about you," James admitted. "I just don't think I want to be married to you right now."

"That sounds like you just said *you don't want me anymore*," Bess said as she turned to stare at him, "and that's the deal breaker. What happened to *through thick and thin?*"

"It's not fair to drag you into my *thick and thin*. It's too much to ask of you," James said shaking his head.

"You're a coward," Bess said lifting her chin. "You might be brave on the battlefield but you're a coward when it comes to love. If you really loved me, you couldn't imagine life without me. I know, because now I have to stop loving you. I can't be your friend. We crossed that line long ago."

James watched as Bess got out of his car. She opened the back door and removed her own suitcase. He watched as she walked up her front porch steps and let herself inside. He stared as she turned on the lights and moved through her rented bungalow.

He knew she was right. He was a coward, afraid to enter into a relationship that would demand all he had to give. He felt too empty, too dead, too exhausted for that kind of give and take intensity. He realized he had nothing left to give. He would spend his time visiting the graves of his fallen brothers, taking care of Ginny till Mike came home. He'd learn to be content with a monthly gathering of the guys. Bess needed more than he could give. She deserved more.

Nineteen

Bess sensed him, sitting in his car watching as she settled back into her life. He stayed for exactly eighteen minutes, his engine on, his eyes looking at her through the window. When he finally pulled out, she smiled realizing, *he does love me. Couldn't pull himself away. He's having a panic attack and flashbacks. He's hyper vigilant to everything going on around him, overloaded, and about to crash.* Bess walked to the stove and turned on her tea kettle. *He forgets that I have PTSD too. I understand what he's going through.*

Bess knew she needed to give him space, remembering the intensity of PTSD attacks. She'd noticed his hands shaking, his eyes monitoring all movement around them while he stood guard over Mitchell's grave. She'd known not to ask what he was thinking and feeling. That would be like asking a drowning man if he wanted a glass of water. She also knew that if he sensed pity, it would put an end to their relationship forever.

Bess fixed her tea, calmed her own emotions, and looked through her purse for the card Marie had slid across the counter while Bess described a plan she was developing. Bess found it, and called the number. When Marie answered, Bess asked, "What does Tim say?"

"He says it's a go. We've already picked out the spot. We might offer to do this for other groups," Marie announced, "if all goes well."

"Great. A man called Russ will be calling in the future. He'll be your contact. I've got to make this all happen. Wish me luck," Bess suggested before hanging up.

Bess looked though her list of numbers and dialed Fran's. When she answered, Bess simply said, "I need to come over. I need to talk to both you and your husband. James needs our help."

"Come right over," Fran answered. "I'll tell Russ you're on your way. We won't make a move until you get here."

Sadie hugged her mom but then pulled away asking, "Why awe you hewe? Didn't you have fun on youw twip?"

"I did," Bess said, before kissing her daughter's cheek. "I need to talk to Miss Fran and Mr. Russ. You still get to spend one more night with Judy."

"Okay," Sadie said, before turning to find her friend.

"I need a glass of wine," Bess admitted, "then I need the three of us to go where we can't be heard. I need your help."

"Let's go to my den," Russ said, leading the way down the hall.

Bess walked into the room, her eyes darting from one snap shot to another. They were all there, the faces of the men from his platoon. "Oh my God," Bess said as she walked directly over to one picture. "There's Mitchell." She studied the picture of James, Mitchell, and Russ standing together next to an Afghan shepherd and his sheep. They were all smiling, despite the belts of bullets over their shoulders and the powerful rifles in their hands. "I knew Mitchell," Bess explained to Russ.

"I know," Russ admitted. "James told me."

"Of course he did," Bess said. "I imagine he tells you almost everything." She smiled affectionately at Russ. "I'm grateful he has you in his life and that you live so close. We need to talk. James needs all our help."

Russ pointed toward the couch, and he sat on his office chair. "Enlighten us," he demanded, his clenched jaw a telltale sign of his concern.

"Russ, you need to know a few things about me. I suffer from PTSD just like James. So does Sadie. We're getting better, but I know the signs of the various symptoms coming on."

Since no words were needed, Russ nodded. Bess continued saying, "I have good news and bad news. The good news is, James asked me to marry him and I said yes!"

Fran jumped to their feet and stood, exclaiming, "Wonderful, wonderful."

"And the bad news?" Russ insisted, his eyes not leaving Bess. "The next morning, at the Bed and Breakfast, James announced our engagement. He was as happy as I was. Two mothers were sitting at the table. They were staying there while they visited their fallen sons at Arlington."

"Oh," Russ said, as he wiped his hand across his own brow.

"It gets worse. They talked about how their sons would never get married and how lost they were without them." Bess stopped, seeing the same look of pain in Russ' eyes as she had seen in James. "I won't go on," Bess said, as she watched Russ turn away and look at various pictures.

"It couldn't have come at a worse time," Russ admitted. "James let his guard down, opened up, and then that happened."

"Yup," Bess agreed.

"Then what?" Russ demanded, his glaze returning to Bess.

"The night before, once we found out how close we were to the National Cemetery, we had made plans to visit Mitchell's grave,"

Bess said. "After what happened at breakfast, I asked if he still wanted to."

"He said he had to," Russ finished, and Bess nodded *yes*.

"Once at Arlington he had a guide mark the grave sites for eight men," Bess said, watching as Russ turned back to the wall of photos. His eyes shifted until he found each of the eight.

"We only went to Mitchell's grave. Ginny called and asked us to come right home. Mike is in that terrible battle on the news. She needed James to be home in case the call came in," Bess said as Russ' eyes retuned to hers.

"What the fuck? Could it get worse?" Russ asked.

"Not much worse," Bess admitted. "James' hands were shaking. I didn't talk on the way home. We listened to the radio."

"Thank God," Russ said. "Thank you for that."

"He's having flashbacks. He was hyper vigilant, the worse time to have to stand there while twenty-one gun salutes were occasionally being fired," Bess said.

"You've got to be kidding," Russ said, staring at Bess.

"What's hyper vigilant?" Fran asked.

"I have it when I get flashbacks. My entire body becomes hypersensitive to any sounds or movements that could be a threat to me or Sadie. Meanwhile, I'm flashing back to fighting the bear, seeing Drew on the ground, and smelling the blood. He was having flashbacks while hearing the rifle fire and the bugles' taps and still he managed to stand perfectly still in his *on-guard stance*."

"That's Cap," Russ said standing up. "I need to go see him."

"Not yet," Bess said, raising one eyebrow. "I have a plan." Bess watched Russ hesitate, take one step toward the door, then decide to sit and listen. "We all need to go over to James' house; Ginny needs to talk to Fran, and I need to talk to James."

"As his future wife, I'm going to suggest the following," Bess explained. "James needs to visit all eight graves, but not alone. Any soldier who wants to should go along. You need to do this together. In addition, I think you need to go on the first Saturday of this month. You can camp on the grounds of the Inn where we stayed. I've already contacted the owners, and they have a back acreage where you are welcome to set up camp. Get a rental truck and take all those tents in the barn down to the Inn. Spend the days visiting the grave sites and the nights camping out, talking together. You all need to do this," Bess said, raising her eyebrow again at Russ.

"Yes, Ma'am, Mrs. Cap," Russ said, with a slight grin, "but it'll be lambing season. You need us to help with the lambing."

"No I don't," Bess said firmly. "I'm going to be the head shepherd on The Funny Farm. Any women and children who want to come help will be welcome. We can all bunk together in the big barn. I plan to have the 4-H Sheep Club come help as well. If they do, the members can pick out a free lamb to raise for their sheep project. We have too many sheep on The Funny Farm. Mitchell would want us to give them to the 4-H kids," Bess decided.

"Yes Ma'am," Russ said standing and walking toward her. "Glad to have you in charge," he said as he crossed over and extended his hand to help her up. "Cap's in for it, isn't he?"

"Yes, he sure is. That man has no idea how loved he's gonna be," Bess said smiling. "I'm going over to see him now. I would like you all to come along. You order pizza for supper, okay Russ?" Bess asked.

"Will do, Mrs. Cap," Russ said, beaming.

"After James and I work things out, I'll need you to assist James with the troop movement to the Inn," Bess explained.

"Happy to do that," Russ said. "No doubt Cap will take charge. It will do him good."

"Shall we move out?" Bess asked, as they both turned to Fran.

"What just happened?" Fran asked.

"Mrs. Cap just took charge. She's got Cap's back," Russ said, chuckling. "She's got one powerful eyebrow."

They arrived together: Bess, Sadie, Judy, and her brother in one car, Fran and Russ in the other. Shep came running to check out the new arrivals, his tail wagging welcome once they were recognized.

When they walked into the farmhouse, they found both Ginny and James slumped in front of the TV. They looked up like defeated captives, confused by the company.

"Did you tell Ginny that we're getting married?" Bess asked, beaming down at him.

"What?" Ginny asked, the light coming back to her eyes.

"Mama, are you reawwy?" Sadie asked, just before jumping onto James' lap. "You did it! You're gonna be my daddy," she yelled, hugging him. "I wove you alweady."

James hugged his new daughter and looked over her shoulder to smile at Bess. He looked so exhausted yet suddenly hopeful.

"If you'll excuse me," Bess said. "I'm going up to the tree house."

"No one but Mr. James is allowed in the tree house," Judy announced.

"No one but Mr. James and his wife are allowed in the tree house," Bess said. "Right, darling?"

James was standing, still holding onto little Sadie. "That's right," he said, beginning to grin. "What's happening?"

"Mrs. Cap has a good plan. I've already been briefed. I'm supposed to order pizza for everyone," Russ said, nodding assurance toward James. "We got this covered. You better get briefed on the rest. It's a good plan, Cap; just watch out when she gives you that eyebrow."

James followed her up the various colored steps, glad he'd put a rail running up along the tree beside them. He was worried she'd fall, grateful she took her time. He stopped, suddenly tired again, and looked out into the field of sheep. They were beautiful but suddenly overwhelming to James. *Six hundred?* he thought. *I'm a fool.*

He noticed Bess stopped when she realized he wasn't following. She was looking out at the sheep as well. "I'd like to be put in charge of the sheep," she called down. "I'm so excited; I've got it all figured out," Bess said before moving up the ladder again.

James felt the heavy load lift from his shoulders. He closed his eyes, took in a deep breath, and felt suddenly refreshed. When he opened his eyes, she was several steps above him. He climbed quickly to catch up, eager to stay close to her.

Nearing the tree house, Bess noticed that James had built the steps to gently bend away from the tree, becoming a wooden staircase leading up to a large deck. Bess followed the steps, reached the deck, and let out a sigh of appreciation. A three-foot wide deck surrounded the tree house, the rail and banisters securing her safety. "This is beautiful, James. More than I could have ever imagined," she said, while waiting for him to reach her side.

He walked to her, placing his arm around her waist. They stared down at the sheep, hearing Rascal begin braying as he ran toward Sadie, Judy, and her brother who were walking toward the field. "We're going to have a wonderful life together," Bess promised, as she turned to gently kiss James' lips.

"I was afraid I lost you. You said I was a *coward*," James said, shuddering at the word.

"The farthest thing from the truth. If you had stepped on the gas and sped away, you might have lost me," Bess explained, "but you sat there, making sure I got in safely. It was then that I knew you truly loved me. You are my hero, my destiny, and the future father of my next three children. I predict another little girl and two sons are in your future. Can you handle that, Captain?"

"More children?" James said, hugging her to him. "Sons and another daughter? Wouldn't that be wonderful? More than a man could ever dare dream of?"

"You deserve happiness. All your fallen soldiers would want that for you. You have to show the other men that it's all right to find happiness, peace, and joy. Show them that a civilian's life can be full of meaning, servitude, and comradeship. After all, this country exists for the civilians. You soldiers fought to give us this life."

"I never thought of that before," James admitted. "I'm so tired, Bess."

"I know, honey. Let me take the lead for a little while. I'm here for you just like you'll be there for me when I need you," Bess said, resting her head on his chest.

"I don't think you need anyone," James said, sighing.

"I'll need you to hold my hand when I'm scared and having one of my PTSD attacks. I have all the symptoms you get. It's exhausting; I know that. I'll need you to hold my hand while I'm delivering our babies, to help when they get sick, to support me when we discipline them. They'll all be a handful, if they take after us."

"They sure will be," James said, laughing and feeling stronger. "I want to show you something inside," he said taking her hand and leading Bess toward the tree house's front door.

Twenty

When the door swung opened, Bess let out a cry of astonish-
ment. It was an artist's studio, but fastidiously organized with
military precision. One tall, wooden bench held tubes of paint,
lined up by hue. Jars of clean, but well used, brushes were
grouped in easy access to the various easels. Drawers filled with
colored chalk and pencils were carefully arranged like the paint,
by color. All the materials were well used, proving this was the
working studio of an artist. This was no hobbyist's corner.

Three large easels contained paintings covered by a muslin
cloth. James walked up to one and gently removed the cloth. There
Sadie stood holding little Millie, in front of the burning fireplace
in his bedroom. Sadie's big, blue eyes looked directly at Bess, her
little lips looked about to say Mama. Bess couldn't breathe, then
suddenly began to weep, her hand reaching out to James for support. He put his arms around her, holding her up as she blub-
bered and leaned against him.

Before she barely gained control, he turned and pulled off
another piece of cloth. Bess turned, as the material fell to the
ground exposing a portrait of her, realistic as the day it had happened. Bess was walking through the rows of chocolate-colored

dirt, the creek flowing behind her. In her arms, wrapped in Sadie's pink coat, were all the kittens. They were mere fluffs of fur but identifiable now that they had grown. The kittens' eyes were still closed, their little faces nuzzling up against the pink material. Bess studied the face of her image. The woman had a curious look of both concern and wonder.

Bess grabbed for James as she whispered, "It's wonderful. More than I could have imagined. When did you do these?"

"I started this one that very day. Bess, this is the moment I fell in love with you," James admitted.

"What's under that cloth?" Bess asked, growing anxious and hopeful for more.

James pulled off the cloth and Bess stared at the painting of herself, using the Shepherd's hook to move the ewe having trouble giving birth. The little head of the lamb was looking out at her, still trapped in her mother's body. Bess looked to find James' image and there it was, helping her adjust the ewe so the lamb could be repositioned for easy delivery. They were working together, as a team, the man looking adoringly at the woman. The red-haired woman was focused only on the lamb.

The studio had a loft, and they climbed onto the queen size mattress and laid down. They stared at the ceiling above them; it had been painted blue with tiny stars and a full moon. She whispered her plan for the visitation to the cemetery and heard his sigh of relief and appreciation. She told him her plans for the April lambing, explaining how she would use it as a chance to teach 4-H members and leaders about lambing and caring for sheep. She assured him the number of her flock would be reduced to only one hundred and she was going to add just fifty more Shetland sheep to offer him a variety of different colored sheep to paint.

"Russ is waiting to talk with you. Should he come up here?" Bess asked, upon completing her discussion.

"No, honey. Only you will ever come up here. I'll build another tree house for our kids, but this is my studio and only you will come here," he explained.

"Our own special place," Bess said. "Someday soon I'll come to have you sketch me naked; we never got around to that." She turned to her side and gently kissed his lips before promising, "I won't invade your studio while you're creating. I'll only come when invited."

He leaned over and kissed her. "I love you very much."

"So what's happening?" Sadie asked, her arms folded across her chest. "Awe we gonna to move into this house?"

"Yes, I'll ask if you can stay in your school until the year is over. It's only a few more months," Bess explained.

"What then?" Sadie asked.

"Then you get to go to Judy's school. Not the same classes; she's older than you,' Bess advised.

"That's good," Sadie decided. "Do I get to keep Miwwie?"

"Of course, not only Millie but all the animals on this farm become yours too," James explained.

"Even Wascal?" Sadie asked hardly able to contain herself.

"Yes, he's yours too," James said, sitting down beside Ginny. "He still needs to guard the sheep."

"But thewe my sheep too," Sadie suggested. All the adults watched as Sadie considered all possibilities. She moved in front of James and asked, "Do I get a pony?"

"A pony," James asked, noticing her little blonde eyebrow raise. "Look Russ, she does it too. I'm in deep trouble." They all laughed.

"Come see my new room," Sadie said to the other kids.

"You don't know which one is yours," Bess exclaimed, shaking her head.

"Oh yes she does. She already told me which one she wants," James explained. "How are you doing, Sis? Any word yet?"

"I just got another email saying we'll be notified as soon as they are out of danger," Ginny said, reading from her iPhone. "What the hell does that mean?"

"It means they're being air lifted out," James said. "Knowing Mike, he'll be the last man to go. He's a stubborn shit," James said, shaking his head.

"When should I start to worry?" Ginny asked, and noticed James look over at Russ. "It's now, right. This is the most dangerous part, when they're getting lifted up into the copters."

"They might already be out of danger," Russ advised. "That email's got to be a good half hour behind."

Only the crackling in the fireplace and the voices of the children upstairs could be heard. All adults were lost in prayer or thoughts of Mike and the soldiers in Afghanistan.

The sound of Ginny's cell phone shattered all concentration. Her eyes wide, her hands shaking, she lifted it and said, "Hello." They watched as she gasped and finally asked, "Is that you? Mike, is it really you?"

While they all celebrated, she rose and walked into her bedroom, her phone to her ear. When she returned, they had trouble reading her body language. Ginny was still shaking, all the color drained from her face. She looked like a woman in shock and they quietly gathered around her once she sat back down on the sofa.

"He's wounded," Ginny announced. "One shot hit him in the arm. He promises it's not bad, worst might be nerve damage. They'll

fly him out to Germany tomorrow, then back home after a few days."
Ginny wiped her tears and smiled, "He's alive! Thank God, he's alive."

"He'll get a Purple Heart. That'll look great on his uniform
when you get married," Russ suggested with a shrug. "He'll match
Cap and about ten other guys in our platoon."

"The wedding won't happen until summer," Ginny added.
"Once they ship him to a hospital stateside, I'm not leaving his
side. I go where he goes." Ginny turned and added, "I told him
about you getting married to Bess. He suggested we make it a dou-
ble wedding. Most of the same people will be going to both. I'd
love that. Brother and sister getting hitched on the same day. Mom
and Dad would love that too."

"It's up to Bess," James said, taking Bess's hand and lifting it to
his lips.

"Perfect," Bess announced. "I'd only be adding a few more
guests: my friends at The Mannings and any 4-H kids that help us
lamb."

The joy came back to Ginny's face. "We'll have five months to
plan it. Dad's giving me away; who'll give you away?" Ginny asked,
growing interested in the wedding plans.

"Sadie," Bess decided. "She'll stand by our sides as we all get
hitched."

"Wonderful," Ginny announced. "Let's talk dresses."

"I'm out of here; how about you?" James said, as Russ and he
walked onto the deck.

In time for the wedding, the farmhouse was painted, each
architectural detail highlighted in a different color. "Like a painted
lady," Bess had explained, when she told James how she'd like her
home to look.

It turned out to be a beautiful day for a wedding, cool for August. Each guest got to pick out a cake of freshly made lavender- or spice-scented goat soap. Two lambs were roasting over a pit rotisserie, two turkeys for those unwilling to eat lamb. The fresh vegetables all came from the garden, as did the fresh herbs that adorned the large archway constructed by his men. Wild violets were laced among the greenery.

A fellow knitter played the harp as the guests arrived. Group pictures were taken of the invited standing next to Rascal, who was adorned in a white collar, black tie, and top hat. Sadie rewarded the donkey periodically with a carrot for his patience. He only bit two men and one woman's purse.

Mike strode among the guests, hugging his former comrades, and reacquainting himself with their families. Ginny glowed, not letting him leave her sight. She wore her mother's wedding gown, shortened so that it came above her knees and showed off her long, lean legs. She looked radiant and sexy.

All the men wore their dress uniforms, medals, and ribbons. It was overwhelming for family and friends to see the decorations these brave soldiers had earned. A guest called the press demanding they take pictures and in no time news cameras showed up to cover the story.

"It's bedlam out there, James warned, as he walked into the farmhouse. "The news truck is doing a live feed. They want you and Ginny out front."

"Let Ginny go," Bess suggested. "Have Mike and Ginny tell them where he was a few months ago. We'll go out in a few minutes."

"Wait, I'll call Ginny and ask her to do the first part of the interview," James said. Completing that task, he turned to stare at his future wife. "You look so beautiful in that lace dress. I can't believe you knit it!"

"Thanks, because I won't be able to wear it for very long. I have a news flash of my own," Bess said, after he completed his call.

"I never know what you're going to say. What new project have you thought of?" James asked.

"I think we need to paint the upstairs bedroom," Bess said, tilting her head.

"We're going to get married in less that fifteen minutes, and you're picking out paint colors for a spare room?" James laughed.

"It's not for a spare room," Bess said, lifting one perfectly shaped eyebrow. "You said you would love to have more children, so I stopped taking my birth control pills. It's going to be a nursery."

He stood perfectly still, his eyes wide, his heart pounding. Finally his lips parted and he muttered, "I remember the day you came striding through the field, rubber boots on your feet, a determined look on your beautiful face. I was terrified, not knowing what to do to save that little lamb whose head was sticking out. You carried a Shepherd's Hook, looking brave, in control and unstoppable. I knew you were my hero, would keep me on the straight and narrow, assist me with any mess I got into, but I never dreamed how wonderful it was going to be. All I knew was, I was hooked."

The End!

Read on for an overview of the Living Passionately Series and the next book being written.

I hope you have enjoyed reading Book One, Racing Desire, and Book Two, The Shepherd's Hook. While writing them, the women in the Living Passionately Series became my closest friends. It is difficult to let them go, but I've already plotted several more books and heroines to replace them.

My goal in the Living Passionately Series is to tell the story of various women who are enthralled with their chosen vocation. The women will be very different but share certain attributes. They will each be imperfect and vulnerable. They will enjoy living in the flow, embracing all life's experiences without hesitation. When love enters their lives, they will run toward it, enthusiastic partners in the exploration of all its mysteries. These women know that only through connections are we truly alive.

Aurora's Glow

Aurora is a stained glass artist, passionate about her historic city, clinging to her childhood memories of friendly streets and well swept sidewalks. While examining a stained glass window she must repair, she meets Blake the craftsman in charge of the renovation. The view outside the window reveals a sickening situation. Together they learn that an abandoned home from her past is now the site of criminal activities. Follow Blake and Aurora as they fall in love and realize a city cannot be saved by merely refurbishing its houses. The city's glow has to be nurtured to reignite its soul. Due out in time for 2014 summer reading.

In the meantime, please consider reading my first series, The Dennison Historical Fiction Family Saga. The three books, Until There Was Us, Rising Up, and Worlds Apart, are very different from each other. They are a tale of people living with gusto through different times and circumstances.

Thank you all for giving me a reason to write.

About the Author

Creative parents raised Pamela Harrison Bender. Someone was always painting, gluing, singing, dancing, or making something. Her father took her to a yarn shop at age ten, bought her enough yarn to make a sweater, and signed her up for knitting lessons. Seeing her self-doubt and rising panic, he repeated their family's mantra, "You can do anything you set your mind to." Pam admitted that she set her mind to making that dog-gone sweater. By the time she graduated from high school, Pam knitted many sweaters, designed and constructed stained-glass windows, wrote several stories, and learned to have faith in her own ability to finish whatever she started

When she retired, Pam and her husband, Joe, traveled around America. On one such trip, her knitting needles were picked up again. That naturally evolved into learning to spin her own yarn from the 100 pounds of raw fleece she bought on a whim from the Crow Indian Reservation in Crow Agency, Montana. Once Pam and Joe became 4-H leaders of their Dying to Knit Club, the never-ending wonders of working with fiber were explored with their club members.

The Shepherd's Hook characters are living passionately, dedicated to their country, their farm, the animals under their care, and the soldiers with whom they served. Bender's respect for their work and her compassion for our returning soldiers from the battlefields is undeniable. The Shepherd's Hook exposes just how difficult their journey home can be.

Read Book:

Juanita Breudenbaugh 6-1-14

Carol LaPorte 9-3-14

Made in the USA
Charleston, SC
06 March 2014